10|03

EDGE
OF
NIGHT

EDGE
OF
NIGHT

•

Cynthia Danielewski

AVALON BOOKS
NEW YORK

PRINTED IN THE UNITED STATES OF AMERICA
ON ACID-FREE PAPER
BY HADDON CRAFTSMEN, BLOOMSBURG, PENNSYLVANIA

Dedicated to my family in appreciation of their support.

Chapter One

The small house on the Long Island Sound was lit like a beacon as the guests from the party began to take their leave. Fog had blanketed the ground and a light drizzle had begun to fall as Lisa Baker, a young graduate student, said good night and began the walk home. Her apartment was just a few short blocks away, and the streets were quiet as she made her way to the building.

Passing the small local cemetery that bordered the park, she kept her eyes carefully averted from the aging tombstones. The cemetery was old and filled to capacity, most of the tombstones and crypts cracked and broken, lending an eerie feel to the hallowed grounds. It was more of a local historical landmark than anything else, but it never failed to chase shivers down her spine whenever she walked by. Tonight was no exception.

Lisa was well past the wrought iron gate that led to the winding road within the cemetery when the creaking sound of it opening caused her to stop dead in her tracks. She listened with her heart in her throat as her eyes, wide and dilated, skimmed the darkness.

The hair on her nape and arms stood on end as she caught sight of a hooded figure in a black flowing robe making its way toward her, its footsteps barely registering in the quiet night. It was too dark to see the figure's face; the hood concealed all remnants of its features. A hint of silver was visible in the darkness.

Lisa kept her eyes trained on the menacing figure that slowly stalked toward her, her mind questioning the reality of the situation. When the robed figure lifted its arm, revealing a dagger that glinted in the moonlit darkness, she didn't take time to ask questions. She ran.

Heart pounding, adrenaline flowing, Lisa felt her feet hit the ground hard as she tried to escape her assailant.

With nowhere to go, no welcoming house in sight, she turned into the park, hoping to get lost in the trees that densely populated the area. The wind hit her in the face, causing her eyes to tear, mixing with the rain that was becoming steadier by the minute. The darkness in the park was suffocating, no moonlight seeped through the treetops that now boasted their spring leaves. Every sound was magnified, every noise terrifying.

Her breathing ragged, Lisa paused near an old oak tree, gripping the trunk for balance while she tried to catch her breath and make sense of where she was and where she could hide.

The snapping of twigs alerted her to the hooded figure's presence before she could see him. Hands pushed out in front of her as if to hold him at bay, she shook her head, unable to scream past the terror that gripped her. She could barely breathe as she slowly edged one foot behind the other, cringing away from the silver dagger that was now raised high in the air. Finding her vocal cords, she let out one terrified scream as the blade arched toward her throat.

Chapter Two

Detective Jack Reeves was sound asleep when the phone rang at 5:30 that morning. Fumbling with the receiver, he brought the handset to his head.

"Yeah," he mumbled groggily, his eyes beginning to close again.

"Jack?" a wide-awake voice boomed over the line.

Jack recognized the voice immediately. It belonged to his partner, Ryan Parks. "Ry? What time is it?" he asked as his eyes tried to adjust to the darkness of the room. His gaze immediately focused on the red glowing numbers of his alarm clock. He let out a string of curses as he registered the time.

Ryan laughed good-naturedly. "It's five-thirty in the morning. Time to rise and shine. Your vacation is officially over."

"This had better be good," Jack warned, automatically turning to stare at his wife of one week. Ashley slept peacefully at his side, undisturbed by the early morning call. They had only arrived home the previous night from their honeymoon, and he knew she was exhausted from the long flight. If the truth were told, he could have used a few more hours of sleep too. The flight time from New York to Hawaii had been bad enough, but when it was combined with a four-hour layover at the crowded San Francisco airport, the trip home had become excruciating.

"Would I call you at this ungodly hour if it wasn't good?" Ryan questioned, his voice full of mock hurt.

Jack closed his eyes and stifled a groan. Though he liked his partner immensely, he hated the fact that he had such a cheerful disposition first thing in the morning. Jack liked to wake up gradually, with no surprises and little talk. "Ryan, it's too early for this. What gives?"

Ryan laughed at Jack's surly tone. He knew from experience that his friend just wasn't a morning person, and he normally tried to keep his tone low key until Jack joined the land of the living. "Okay, okay, calm down. The reason I called is to let you know that there's been another murder."

"So?" Jack asked, not seeing the importance of the statement. They worked homicide. Murder was their job.

"Not a typical murder," Ryan replied. "The body was found by the old cemetery near the Sound."

Jack rubbed a tired hand across his eyes as he sat

up in bed, the sheet falling to his waist. "Maybe the killer thought it was an appropriate place to dump a body," he said off-handedly, almost cold-heartedly. Working homicide had definitely given him an edge of cynicism. The cynicism wasn't directed at the victim, however, only at the suspects. He had found out early on that for the most part, there was little value placed on life in general. The murderers placed no value on it, and lately it seemed that even the police department took death for granted. He supposed it was only natural, when you worked around it every day, but he personally thought it was a shame to become so jaded.

Jack took his job seriously. Finding a murderer and putting him or her away for good had become the main focus of his life. Even if it meant bending the rules to do it. He saw nothing wrong with going outside the law to solve a case. Sometimes there was just no other way to go about it. It seemed at times as if the criminals had all the rights and the victims and their families had none. Experience had taught him that. And he knew from experience that there was no room for weakness in solving the cases he was assigned to. Everybody was a suspect. Everybody had to be a suspect until there was no room for doubt.

"You can be so cold-hearted at times, Jack. I wonder what Ashley sees in you," Ryan ribbed. He knew Jack's attitude made him good at his job. And while it might not win him any humanitarian awards, he did have a knack for solving the cases.

"So tell me what's so special about this case," Jack demanded, stretching his folded hands out in front of him until he heard the cracking of his knuckles. He settled back against the pillows, the receiver tucked between his shoulder and neck.

"The body was found in a shallow grave," Ryan answered, the words falling like dead weight into the darkness of the morning.

Jack immediately sat upright, his full attention on what was now being said. "In a grave?"

"Yeah, a fresh one. There was no dirt covering it, so I'm not sure if they just didn't have time, or if it's supposed to be symbolic or something."

"Was it drug related?" Jack immediately questioned, grasping at the one thing he knew was usually a common denominator in cases such as this. His mind immediately shifted into gear as he began going over everything that was said.

"I don't know if she was a user or not. There's no concrete evidence on the scene to suggest it. We'll have to wait for the autopsy report to come in," Ryan replied. "So are you coming down or what?"

Jack glanced at the bedside clock once again. "I'll meet you there within the hour."

"I'll bring some coffee," Ryan promised before hanging up the phone.

Jack reached out to place the receiver back in the cradle. He sat in bed for a moment, wondering what it was about his job that kept him going. He hated seeing the bodies for the first time, seeing the frozen expression on the victim's face, often showing traces of a terror so intense that he had difficulty imagining what the final seconds of life had been like. Even more, he hated contacting the next of kin.

More times than not, he made arrangements to meet them at the morgue, hoping to soften the grief. But there was just no way to prepare them for the first glimpse of their loved one's still form. He always found himself looking away from the open devastation that was visible in their eyes and body language. He dreaded having to face the despair once again, but he also knew that he couldn't walk away from it. He wasn't able to. He didn't know what force pulled him to the job, he only followed it. He had already tried once to walk away, only to fail.

Jack kept the bedside lamp turned off as he made his way into the adjoining bathroom to take a quick shower. Looking into the mirror, he pushed a careless hand through his black hair that was just now beginning to show signs of gray. Though he was close to forty, his lifestyle had aged him. A long deep scar ran from his temple to his mouth, lending a sinister air to his already heavily lined face. The scar was compliments of his first case in the homicide division.

At the time, a popular slasher movie had just been released at the theaters, and a mentally unstable teenager had decided to copycat the theme. Jack had underestimated the kid and had tried to reason with him, hoping to bring him in without force or violence. The kid's parents had pleaded with him not to harm their son. Jack had let his compassion for them interfere with his job. It had almost been a fatal mistake on his part, and was one he would never repeat. That the kid was now dead held no appeasement. The scar was a constant reminder that he could never afford to let his guard down.

He leaned against the vanity, studying the bearded shadow that now graced his jaw. Running an experimental hand over it, he debated whether to shave. He was bone-weary tired. Tired from his trip, tired of seeing death, and just sometimes tired of life in general.

Jack looked through the partially open door and saw Ashley's still form sprawled on the bed in a peaceful sleep. The sight brought a glimmer of a smile to his face. If somebody had told him a year ago that he would be married a second time, he would have laughed in the person's face. He had tried it once before, with disastrous results. He had learned early on that commitment was the equivalent of suffocation. His ex-wife was a clinging vine who was jealous of everything in Jack's life, including his career. The stress of the relationship had taken its toll and the marriage didn't make it beyond a couple of years. Jack wasn't into failure, never had been. One mistake was all he was willing to risk in this lifetime. Until Ashley.

He had met her at a press conference. She was a bulldog of a reporter who wanted answers that he was unwilling to give about a case. She had dogged his steps relentlessly, seeking her story. At first he thought she was nothing but a royal pain, and he would have given his eyeteeth to lock her up just to get her off his back. But eventually, something changed between them. Jack could remember the exact moment.

It was when he was called in to investigate a murder scene that involved a child. Ashley had arrived simultaneously. He had felt a dark rage at seeing her there, wondering if she got a thrill from death. That she had connections with somebody on the force who had leaked the information was obvious. It was the only explanation to why she consistently arrived when the police arrived. It was an annoying habit of hers, and he had never been able to discover her source. To this day, she wouldn't even tell him. He admired her dedication and loyalty, but the look in her eyes that night as she caught the first glimpse of the child was frightening, bone chilling. Jack never again thought that she was a thrill seeker. He now knew that she honestly believed the public had a right to know what was going on in the community. At times he agreed with her. Forewarned was forearmed. But he couldn't help but believe that in that particular case, ignorance would have been bliss for her.

Jack knew it wasn't just seeing the scene that prompted her look of distress. It had to be something more. It didn't take much for her to open up. He learned that night that he wasn't the only one with a disastrous marriage behind him. She had one too. She had another secret as well. Her kid sister had been raped and murdered, and she was reliving the incident that night. Jack knew at that moment that he would gladly give his life to ensure that look was never again on her face. That was the beginning for them.

The slamming of a car door outside brought him out of his reverie. He reached for his electric razor and began to run it over his beard. Once satisfied with the smoothness of the shave, he adjusted the water temperature in the shower before stepping under the stinging spray.

Several minutes later, he reentered the bedroom, a towel knotted at his waist and a cloud of steam following in his wake.

"Jack?" a soft voice whispered from the bed.

Jack paused by the closet and turned to look through the darkness at his wife. "What, babe?"

Ashley sat up in bed, her blond hair tousled as she squinted through the darkness trying to focus on her newly acquired husband. "Where are you going? What time is it?"

"It's early yet. Go back to sleep," he murmured as he took a suit and dress shirt out of the closet.

She studied him though the darkness, noticing the shadows under his eyes, the whiteness of the scar that ran from his temple to his jaw. She knew the scar bothered him, not because of the physical defect, but because he believed that the reason he bore it was because he failed to trust his instincts. He had let compassion override common sense, and he had paid. He didn't know that it was the scar that had made her see him in a different light, in a human light. She longed to reach out to him, to trace his features. She loved everything about this man. Sometimes she worried that he had no clue just how important he was to her. She sensed his tension and knew without being told that there had been another murder. "Won't you at least tell me where you're going?" she asked, her voice full of the persistence that made her so good at her career.

Jack opened a dresser drawer and removed a pair of dress socks. "Ryan called. I have to go out," he told her as he walked back into the bathroom to finish getting dressed.

When he came back into the bedroom, he sat on the edge of the bed to put on his shoes. He felt his wife absently run her hand across his back.

"There's been another murder," she said, the sentence a statement and not a question. She slowly rubbed the tension from his muscles, feeling them bunch beneath her roaming hand.

"Yes," he affirmed, without further comment. He wanted nothing more than to crawl back into bed with her, but he knew he wouldn't. He knew he couldn't. Ryan was waiting.

"I'm sorry," she whispered, knowing how he felt the first time he saw a body. She had always watched his face whenever she was at a crime scene with him, unable to explain the magnetism that drew her to him. She knew what his job took from him emotionally. She also knew that there wasn't another person in this world who could read him, who understood just what it did to him.

"So am I," he replied. He turned around and trapped

her in his arms. He stared at her a moment as if memorizing her features. It bothered him sometimes that he had such a depth of feeling for this woman. He didn't know what he would do if anything ever happened to her. Lowering his head, he rested his forehead against hers before placing a light kiss on her parted lips. "It's early. Try to go back to sleep."

"I can come with you," she offered, waiting for the denial she knew he would give.

Jack looked down at her eyes, his hands absently caressing her hair. "We've already had this conversation. Your days of covering homicide are over. I don't want you on the crime scenes anymore."

"Tom asked me to reconsider my decision of moving to the Op-Ed department," she told him tentatively, trying to read his expression as her words registered. She hadn't meant to tell him this way, knowing how he felt about her covering the police beat. Some of their earlier confrontations over the matter had resembled a war zone.

Jack looked at her for a brief moment, stunned by the statement. Tom Black was Ashley's editor, and it was no surprise that the man would fight tooth and nail to keep his star reporter. Only a fool would let go of her without a fight, and the man was no fool. Jack had met him several times, and instantly disliked him. Partly because of his job—police and news agencies rarely mixed—but the close friendship Tom had with Ashley bothered him more. "Black asked you to give up your chance to write the column?" Jack asked in disbelief.

"He just asked me to reconsider my decision. He's not forcing the issue. He gave me my start at the paper, and he knows what I'm capable of."

Jack wasn't paying attention to her words, his mind going over the ramifications of what she was telling him. He hadn't expected her comment. As far as he knew, she had already moved over to the Op-Ed department. He remembered her excitement when she had told him of her chance to write a weekly column. She had seemed satisfied with the arrangement. They had even gone out to dinner to celebrate the new milestone in her career. He knew all along that her first love was reporting; they had spent nights talking about it, often arguing. But he had honestly thought she welcomed the new path in her career. And if the truth were told, he was relieved. He knew he couldn't deal with her being involved with the seedier side of life once they were married. He had tried to explain that he had enough on his plate without constantly worrying if she was okay and out of harm's way. He didn't need that distraction in his life. He couldn't afford it while on the job. Distraction could mean death. He had thought that she understood. He had thought that they had come to a compromise. "I thought we had settled all of this already. I thought you wanted your own column."

"I do. I'm very excited about the idea. But I also

love covering the hard stories. It's what I do best. I thought you understood that."

Jack's facial expression softened at her words. "I do understand that, babe. And it's the fact that you are so good at your job that makes me nervous. You have absolutely no fear when it comes to covering stories. You rush into situations that even a seasoned cop hesitates to go into. I thought you understood my feelings on the subject. I need to be able to do my job without the complication of worrying about you."

Ashley reached out to touch his hand. "I do understand your feelings. And believe me, I'm not trying to diminish their importance. But reporting is in my blood. It's what I love. It's what I'm good at."

"Maybe you'll love writing the column. You haven't even given it a chance yet."

"Maybe," she agreed with a hint of hesitation. She had no doubt that she could do the job; she wouldn't have accepted the offer if she felt she would have any difficulty in adjusting to her new position at the paper. She just couldn't help but wonder if she had made the right decision. Would she have the same knack for writing a weekly column as she did for reporting?

Jack heard the slight uncertainty in her tone and smiled down at her reassuringly. He knew it would be hard for her to make the change. She had dedicated most of her adult life to reporting, and had built a solid reputation covering crime stories. She was now going down an uncharted path, and though he had no doubts that she would make the transition easily, he could understand her reluctance. Wanting to reassure her, he leaned down to kiss her. "I predict that you'll be great at it," he told her softly as he caressed her cheek. He cast a quick glance at the bedside clock, hating the fact that he had to leave her. He wanted time to talk to her. "I have to go. I'll call you later," he whispered, giving her one final kiss before leaving the bedroom.

As Jack walked down the hallway, Ashley's comment about how Black had asked her to reconsider her decision played through his mind. He wouldn't admit it to her, but it had hit him with the force of a sledgehammer. He knew Black made the request because Ashley was great at her job. If the truth were told, she was probably one of the best. But knowing that didn't lessen the impact the words had on him.

He had thought that the matter had been settled. It was obvious that he had been wrong. And somehow, even now, he knew the matter was far from over. It wasn't in Ashley's nature to let things ride, and it was apparent that she was having doubts about leaving reporting for good. The reality of it hit him hard. He regretted that she had chosen that moment to tell him that Black had asked her to reconsider. He hated having any sort of distraction while working. He knew that they would have to reopen the discussion tonight, if only to clear the air.

Jack walked into the kitchen that was illuminated by the overhead stove light. He was relieved to find that the automatic timer on the coffeepot had begun. Reaching for a mug, he held it beneath the steady stream of liquid. He filled it to the rim before taking his first fortifying sip. He felt the beginning of a headache coming on and reached into the cabinet for the aspirin bottle that was always on hand. He popped a few, washing them down with the hot liquid. After gulping down several quick cups of coffee, he headed out into the early morning chill.

Chapter Three

Jack cracked his window as he drove through the black wrought iron gates that led to the old cemetery. The morning was dark and windy for the month of April, with the distinct chill normally reserved for the fall months. Though daylight was breaking, no sunlight showed through the gray clouds that hovered ominously in the sky. A heavy rain had poured the night before, leaving the world looking like it had been through a wash cycle that had failed to spin dry. The bright green leaves that were beginning to appear on the trees glistened with the moisture from the storm.

As he drove farther along the road, the flashing red lights of the patrol cars became visible. Parking his own car, Jack opened the door and stepped out, momentarily disconcerted as a stinging wind hit his eyes. He heard the fierce wind before it whipped through the old trees that lined the winding road, tearing the spring leaves off their branches and whisking them carelessly through the air. Grabbing his suit jacket from the back seat, he shrugged into it before making his way to a group of police officers.

His steps slowed as he approached the officers, his eyes automatically focusing on the still form that rested in a shallow grave. A black plastic sheet had been placed over the body, to keep potential onlookers from seeing too much.

Jack took a deep breath before crouching down. His hand reached for the corner of the plastic, and he slowly lifted the covering back. A single chill raced down his spine as he took in the sight. He stared as if mesmerized at the body of the young woman lying on the ground, her hands folded together as if in prayer. She almost appeared asleep. If it weren't for her crimson-stained clothes, you could almost believe she was resting. As always, he felt a stirring of anger at the waste of life. He had worked homicide for the past ten years, but he just couldn't get used to the total disregard for life that some people had.

The sound of somebody clearing his throat brought Jack out of his reverie. Turning, he saw his partner, Ryan Parks, making his way over. Though Ryan dressed conservatively, his hair was long and clubbed in the back, a holdover from his days in the narcotics division. On somebody in his twenties, the style was barely acceptable. On somebody past the age of fifty, the style was ludicrous. Ryan was fifty-two.

"What do you think?" Ryan asked, motioning with his chin to the body. His gray-streaked brown hair whipped around his face. He carried two cups of coffee, one of which he offered to Jack.

"I think you should get a haircut."

Ryan sighed. "I meant about the murder."

Jack placed the covering over the still form and stood. He shrugged and rubbed a weary hand over the back of his neck, feeling the tension begin to build. "How long have you been here?" he asked, sidestepping the question. Taking a sip of his coffee, he grimaced at its bitterness before placing the cup on the ground by his feet. He reached inside his jacket for the cigarettes that he always kept on hand.

"Not long. I just arrived a few minutes before you did. The cops who arrived first did a good job of securing the area. The technicians collected a lot of samples so far. Hopefully some of it will turn out to be evidence," Ryan said as he reached for the cigarette that Jack offered. He noticed the way Jack had rubbed the back of his neck. "You still get the headaches?" he asked, his voice laced with concern.

Jack cursed himself for letting the weakness show. He hated any sign of sympathy. "Yeah," he answered as he lit his cigarette, cupping his hand around the flame before handing the lighter to Ryan.

"What did the doctor say?"

Jack gave a humorless laugh. "What's there to say? Try and stay off the caffeine, avoid stress. It's easier said than done."

"I see your point," Ryan said, his eyes taking in the group of technicians combing the outside area, searching for evidence. "Man, what a thing to wake up to."

"Yeah, I could think of better ways."

"The captain should be here soon. I called him before I called you, just in case you weren't back from your trip yet," Ryan said.

"We got home about nine last night."

"How did everything go? Was the weather okay?"

"It was Hawaii," Jack responded.

"Those things are going to kill both of you one day," a gruff voice interceded.

Jack and Ryan turned simultaneously to stare at the police captain, Joe Myers. "This and everything else under the sun," Jack replied cynically.

"What did you come up with?" Captain Myers asked.

Ryan lifted one shoulder philosophically. "Not much, I'm afraid. I took the call this morning. I couldn't sleep, so I went down to the station to fill out some paperwork. The original call came in about three forty-five. The caretaker called reporting a disturbance that he didn't feel comfortable investigating. I can't say I blame him. I don't think I would be too willing to walk around the grounds of a cemetery to find out what was disturbing the peace. God knows what you would find," he said with an exaggerated shudder.

"What do we know about the victim?" Jack asked, finishing his cigarette and throwing the butt into his rapidly cooling coffee.

Ryan shrugged. "Her name's Lisa Baker. She was at a friend's party last night and declined a ride home, preferring to walk. She was studying for her master's in anthropology at the state university, but other than that, we have nothing."

"Where's the caretaker?" Jack asked, his eyes scanning the sea of people that were meticulously combing the cemetery grounds.

"In his house, trying to stay out of the way. He already gave his statement to some officers. Other than hearing the commotion, he claims he doesn't know anything."

"Did he mention hearing any voices? Maybe an accent of some type or a specific speech pattern?" Jack asked.

Ryan shook his head. "No. He couldn't identify the sounds. Looking at the scene, he probably heard the shovel hit the ground. Why? What's your theory?"

"An execution," Jack replied.

The captain walked around the shallow grave before crouching down to lift the tarp. He studied the victim. "You think this could be a hit?"

Jack shrugged. "It was a clean kill, leaving no margin of error. Think about it. There was no way this girl could have survived to identify her attacker. Her vocal cords were severed, along with her jugular. It was bloody, but it was definitely thorough."

Myers nodded as he considered the possibility. "I'll have a complete background check done on her as soon as I get back to my office. If she was involved in something that would shed some light on this, it'll show up."

"Let's hope so. If not, we'll have to look in a different direction," Jack said.

Ryan looked at him curiously. "What direction is that?"

Jack ran a hand through his hair and shrugged. The first thought that had entered his mind upon seeing the crime scene was that it resembled a scene from a low-budget horror movie. The way the body had been laid out, the setting, it was almost as if the murderer was trying to set the stage for a play dealing with the supernatural. And though Jack didn't believe in that type of garbage, he was well aware that there were many people who did. Without blinking an eye, he asked, "Have you heard any rumors about any cults in the area?"

"Cults?"

"Yeah. This isn't your typical murder. Whoever did this went to great pains to lay out the body in a specific way. It has to have some sort of meaning to the killer. If it wasn't a creative hit, it's possible we're dealing with something else entirely different."

Ryan shook his head. "I don't know. I haven't heard about anything strange going on. We've never really investigated anything of that sort. I thought things like that only happened out in the Midwest in the corn fields or something like that."

Jack laughed. "Sometimes I think your ponytail is

too tight. That's like saying that all the people who live in Florida are retired."

"You mean they're not all retired?" Ryan shot back.

"Would you two get serious?" Myers asked with a sigh.

"I'm totally serious," Jack replied. "I don't think we should rule out cult activity, if nothing shows on the other end of the spectrum. It's a growing phase throughout the country, and lord knows there are enough unstable people in this world seeking some type of spiritual meaning and acceptance by their peers. Whether they get it from organized religion or a cult of some sort is immaterial to them."

Ryan looked at Jack doubtfully. "I still don't know. I haven't heard of any sacrifices or anything of that nature being reported recently."

"It doesn't have to be a sacrifice. It could just be symbolic, or a ritual of some sort," Jack replied.

"I don't recall anything that could even be remotely related to that theory," Ryan said.

"Not even in the neighboring towns?" Jack asked. "It doesn't have to be in our jurisdiction. You know as well as I do that crime patterns have a tendency to travel to a different location if the situation gets too hot. Only serial killers looking for immortality in the press will stay in one place. And that's more for a psychological edge than anything else."

Ryan rubbed the bridge of his nose with his thumb and forefinger as he tried to recall if anything strange had been reported. "I can't think of a thing that we could tie this to. Last Halloween a group of teenagers tried to rob a grave at this cemetery, but if I recall, it was only on a dare. I didn't pay any attention to it, figuring it was just a kid's prank."

"That was a sick prank," Myers said, his voice full of disgust. "I remember that story. They never did catch up with the culprits, but no push was ever placed on the case. Like Ryan said, I think they figured it was just a kids' prank that got out of hand. And since they never actually robbed the grave, I guess the case was just sort of buried away in the filing cabinet."

Jack looked around the cemetery, searching for anything out of the ordinary. "You don't happen to remember whose grave they were trying to rob, do you?"

Ryan shook his head. "No, I would have to check the records down at the station. We weren't assigned to the case, so I didn't follow it too closely. Why? Do you think this murder and the crime are related?"

Jack shrugged. "I don't know. I just don't want this murder to be the one that's going to start a string of them."

"If it does turn in that direction, it will be a little different from what we're used to, won't it?" Ryan asked.

"What do you mean?" Jack asked.

"Usually the cases we investigate lead inevitably to drug usage. We haven't found anything here to suggest that she was either a user or a dealer."

Jack shrugged. "Like you said earlier, the jury's out

until we get the autopsy report. We really don't have any idea of what we're dealing with yet. Have they collected any evidence that we could go on that you know of? Or do we have to wait for the samples to be tested before we have any answers?"

"Some fibers from a garment, but that's about it. They're sending them to the lab for investigation. We should know something by late afternoon," Ryan said before falling silent as the coroner's van pulled up to the site.

Jack stood back as the body was lifted from the grave and placed in a black body bag. The sound of the zipper closing grated on his nerves. He couldn't help but study the coroner's face as the body was put in the van. So unemotional, as if the death of one so young was commonplace. Jack once again felt the weariness that had been plaguing him, and he shook off the feeling. He heard the back door of the van close with a cold finality, and he watched the vehicle pull away until the taillights faded in the distance. He turned back to Myers as he heard him speak.

"Do we know if she has any family?" Myers asked.

Ryan shrugged and motioned to a group of people standing off to one side. "They were with her last night at a party. As far as they knew, she had no family. We'll run a computer check though, just to be on the safe side."

Myers nodded. "I'll take care of it. If nothing shows up, I'll have them rush the autopsy."

"How quickly do you think they'll be able to do

it?" Jack asked, once again reaching for his cigarettes. He had been trying to quit, or at least slow down, but all of his good intentions flew out the window the moment a new case came in. His energy level flowed at its highest while he was working, and smoking gave him something to do when he was forced to wait for results. His latest physical had not been good. The doctor had warned him to try to keep stress at bay, but Jack found that smoking was the only thing that seemed to take the edge off.

Myers watched Jack light his second cigarette in five minutes, and shook his head in despair. He wanted to tell Jack that he was slowly killing himself, but he didn't dare. He knew Jack had to make the decision to quit on his own. "The autopsy? With any luck, to-day. Unless extenuating circumstances exist, we should know something by late this afternoon."

"Good. At least we'll have something to go on," Jack replied.

"Yeah," Myers responded. "You two feel like going out to the university to see if there are any leads there? Maybe this is an isolated case. Maybe our killer is somebody she knows from school."

Jack nodded. "I already thought of that. Ryan and I will head over and check it out as soon as we're through here."

"Okay," Myers replied. "Now that I know it's in safe hands, I'm going to head back to my office. I have a meeting with Internal Affairs at ten and I want to go over some notes before I meet with them."

"We'll check in with you later in the day," Jack promised as he watched the captain walk away.

Ryan waited until Myers got into his car before turning to Jack and asking, "What's the matter?"

Jack stepped back as a team of technicians began combing the dirt in the grave where the body had lain. "Nothing. Why?"

Ryan shrugged. "I don't know. You seem preoccupied."

"Just thinking."

"About what?"

Jack shook his head. "About how normal all of this seems to everybody we work with. Almost as if it's commonplace."

Ryan frowned, not understanding where the comment had come from. "People can't afford to get emotionally involved. Nobody would be able to do their job if they were."

"Yeah, I know. That's what makes the whole thing so sad," Jack replied.

"It does get to you after awhile," Ryan acknowledged, stepping back as the technicians gathered trace evidence.

"Some days are worse than others," Jack said softly, almost to himself.

"Everything else okay?" Ryan asked, knowing that something else was bothering his partner.

"What do you mean?"

"As I said, you seem preoccupied," Ryan stated.

"Everything's fine," Jack replied.

"If you ever need to talk, I'll listen."

"Yeah, I know. Thanks."

"I mean it, Jack."

"Everything's okay," Jack assured him before changing the subject. "Well? Should we head over to the school now or wait until later?"

Ryan glanced at his watch. "It's early yet. Do you think we'll have any luck talking to anybody?"

Jack shrugged. "Classes should begin at eight o'clock. People are wrapping up everything here. There's no reason why we shouldn't head over."

"I'm game," Ryan replied.

"Good, let's go and talk to the caretaker before heading out. I want to get a reading on him, just to see what kind of person we're dealing with," Jack said.

"Okay. I wanted to speak with him myself when I got here, but I didn't get a chance," Ryan admitted.

"You didn't get a chance to speak with him at all?"

"No. My attention was diverted as soon as I arrived. One of the other officers questioned him."

"Then let's go meet this guy," Jack said as he turned toward the caretaker's cottage.

Chapter Four

The drive over to the university that morning was done in stop-and-go traffic. Part of the expressway had been closed off due to construction in the early morning hours, and there had been a long delay in opening the lanes in time for the morning rush hour. Consequently, tempers were frayed as traffic moved bumper to bumper past the sight. Horns blared and curses were shouted by numerous drivers running late to work.

"Another construction project that will take years to complete," Jack murmured, his voice full of aggravation.

"You can say that again. This is the only place I know where working construction on the roads is considered having job security," Ryan said.

"It could be worse. At least we don't have to travel this way on a daily basis," Jack replied.

"Yeah. So tell me, what did you think of the caretaker?" Ryan asked, as they waited in the traffic.

Jack shrugged. They had left the crime scene right after talking to the caretaker. Jack felt better after speaking with him, not because they gained any new insight on the events that had transpired that morning, but because he always liked to cover all of the bases. It was too easy for little details to go unnoticed. Details that could mean the difference between solving the murder or the case being stored away in a dusty file cabinet for years, untouched. "I don't know. He didn't appear to be hiding anything."

Ryan nodded. "I got the same impression. He came across as honest and straightforward."

"Mm," Jack murmured. "The only thing I can't understand is why he didn't even look out his window when he heard the commotion outside. For somebody in charge of the grounds, you would think that would be the natural reaction."

"I don't know. I don't think I would look out the window if I was in the same situation," Ryan said.

Jack laughed. "Who are you kidding? Your hair would turn white if you ever had to spend the night in a cemetery. You can't go by what your reaction would be, since there's no chance of you taking a job like that."

"You got that right."

"I know I do. And that being the case, I still want to know why he didn't even look out his blinds."

Ryan's brow furrowed as he considered Jack's words. "You think he's involved in some way?"

"Maybe. I think it's worth running a background check on the man. Better safe than sorry."

"I'll have it run just as soon as we get back to the precinct. It might be interesting to see what comes up."

Jack motioned with his chin to the cell phone that rested on the dashboard. "Why don't you call now and have them start the process? That way, we'll be able to look at it as soon as we get back to the station."

"Okay," Ryan replied as he reached for the phone. It didn't take long to make the request and he placed the phone back on the dashboard when he was done.

"Any problems?"

Ryan shook his head. "It'll be ready when we get there."

"Good."

The traffic slowly began to clear and the car gradually picked up speed. Jack flicked on the turn signal as soon as they reached the exit for the university. He followed the steady stream of traffic to the winding road that led to the campus. The day was overcast, and numerous raindrops fell from the still saturated trees that arched over the road, splattering on the windshield. The sound of the wipers as they cleared the moisture from the glass was the only sound that penetrated the interior of the car. The traffic was surprisingly heavy as students and faculty began their day.

Jack followed the procession of cars turning onto the campus grounds. He parked the car by the administration building and turned to look at Ryan. "What did you say she was studying?"

Ryan reached for his seat belt clip and released the catch. "Anthropology. Why?"

Jack shook his head. "No reason. Just curious. If I remember correctly, that's the study of people. Maybe it'll lead somewhere. Right now, we have a murder and nothing else to go on."

"Yeah, I'm hoping that this will lead somewhere too. The way the body was laid out at the cemetery bothers me. Something just doesn't add up," Ryan responded.

"You think something's going to come out of whatever evidence they were able to get this morning? It didn't look like they picked up much. Mostly evidence that'll have DNA on it. Unfortunately, if we don't find a suspect, there will be nothing to compare it to."

Ryan shrugged. "I don't know. We should have some idea of which direction we need to go by this afternoon. Hopefully, with a little luck, we'll be able to get a partial piece of the puzzle."

"It would be nice if we could put this one to bed early. I'm curious as to what's going to come out of the victim's background check. She looked clean-cut, but looks are sometimes deceiving. For all we know, she went home to a sugar daddy every night. It'll be a lot easier to solve this case if there's something lurking around in her past," Jack said, reaching for his door handle and opening the door. "I think we should start with the administration building. They should be able to point us in the right direction."

"Fine with me," Ryan agreed, stepping out of the vehicle.

They walked over to the administration building, jockeying between students rushing to get to their classes. The walk was brief and they entered the dimly lit corridor that led to the offices.

"You would think that with the price of tuition, they would be able to afford electricity," Ryan said as he removed his sunglasses and placed them in his shirt pocket. The only light that illuminated the hall was the sunlight filtering through the glass doors and windows. The walls were a dingy white, drab and dirty, and a lone janitor was buffing the floors. The smell of disinfectant permeated the air.

"I hate the scent of disinfectant," Jack growled.

"Why? It smells like a hospital. At least you know the place is clean," Ryan returned.

"They should at least open some windows and let the place air out," Jack said.

Ryan laughed. "Quit complaining. It could be worse. Remember our last case? That rat-infested building? I swear those people were using the elevator as a public restroom. This is like taking a walk in the park."

"That place should have been condemned by the

Board of Health years ago. The only purpose it served was as a crack house. The people who lived there were so doped up, half of them couldn't tell you whether it was night or day," Jack said.

"I'll take the smell of disinfectant any day over that. I think I'll remember that place until my dying day. In all my years on the force, that was the worst place I've ever been in. How people can live that way is beyond me," Ryan grumbled.

"They live that way because they're too strung out on drugs to care," Jack returned harshly.

"I realize that. It just always amazes me that people allow drugs to take such total control of their lives, to the point of dictating where and how they live. Even a user crashes to earth eventually. You would think that their living conditions would be a wake-up call," Ryan said.

"You worked narcotics long enough to know that for a lot of people, there is no wake-up call."

"I know. It doesn't make it any easier to understand, though. I have to be honest, I don't miss anything about those days," Ryan admitted before changing the subject. "I wonder how come the hall is so empty, when outside was so busy. You would think that this building especially would have people milling around."

"It's early. I guess most of the people haven't arrived at work yet," Jack responded, reaching up to remove his own sunglasses as they came upon a doorway that led to an office.

They entered the office and walked up to the counter where a young female student was working. She looked up at them as they approached. "Can I help you?"

Jack took out his badge and flipped it open, identifying himself. "I'm Detective Jack Reeves and this is Detective Ryan Parks. We're looking for some information on a student. Lisa Baker. I'm wondering if you could help us."

"Lisa Baker?" the girl repeated, paling by several shades.

"Do you know her?" Jack questioned, his eyes narrowing slightly at the girl's uneasiness.

"I heard she was murdered last night," she murmured, her voice low and barely audible. Her hands had begun to tremble and she quickly took them off the counter and hid them out of sight.

Jack noticed the gesture and studied her curiously. As far he knew, there had been no news vans at the cemetery that morning. He didn't understand how she could have heard about it so quickly, unless she was close to the victim. "May I ask who you heard that from?"

"I was at the same party she was at last night," the girl admitted. "One of the other students called me with the news early this morning. Needless to say, I was shocked. You hear about this kind of thing happening to other people, but never to anybody you know personally."

"What can you tell us about her, Miss . . . ?" Ryan

questioned, pausing and waiting for her to give her name.

"Jones. Mariah Jones."

"Ms. Jones, you said you were at the party last night with Lisa Baker?" Jack asked, studying her from beneath hooded eyes, searching for any sign of distress that seemed unnatural.

"That's right. There were eight of us there. We were celebrating the fact that we would be graduating this spring."

"You were celebrating a little early, weren't you?" Ryan inquired, knowing that finals were still pending.

Mariah shook her head. "Not really. There isn't a reason in the world why any of us would fail. It's a shame about Lisa. She had such a bright future ahead of her. She was going to go on for her doctorate. Why anybody would want to kill her is beyond me."

"Did she have any enemies around campus? Anybody that would want to harm her?" Jack asked.

"No, not that I know of. I can give you a list of her classes and you can check with her professors. Maybe they know something. The truth is, I only knew Lisa on a casual basis. I'm friends with one of her friends."

Jack nodded. "If you would give us a copy of her schedule, we would appreciate it."

"Sure, no problem," Mariah replied before printing out a copy of Lisa's schedule. She handed it over to Jack. "I hope this helps."

"Thank you. We appreciate your assistance in this matter," Jack answered before turning toward the door.

Ryan murmured his own thanks before following Jack outside. "Well? What do you think?" he asked, once the door had closed behind them.

"About her?"

"Yeah."

"I don't know. She appeared a little nervous, but nothing really out of the ordinary. Most people freak out a little bit when confronted by the police. It must have something to do with guilty consciences about other things in their past, like traffic violations or something."

Ryan laughed. "That's true. Do you want to split up the schedule? I can go and interview half and you can do the remainder. We'll make better time that way."

"Sounds good," Jack replied, carefully folding the schedule with a tight crease so that it ripped apart neatly and easily. "Here," he said, handing a portion to Ryan. "You take this half, and I'll look into the other half. With any luck, we'll turn up something."

"I'll meet you back at the car when I'm done," Ryan said before turning and walking in the opposite direction.

"Okay." Jack started down the hall, impatient to uncover a lead, no matter how small.

An hour later, they met up again. Jack was leaning against the bumper of the car, smoking a cigarette, when Ryan walked up.

"Well?" Jack asked, taking a drag off the filter.

Ryan shook his head. "Nothing. The way they

talked about her, you would think she was a saint. It doesn't appear that she ever did anything wrong. Everybody was singing her praises."

"Yeah, I got the same story. It sounds too good to be true. Nobody can be that perfect."

"I agree."

"There has to be something more here than meets the eye."

"Yeah, but what?" Ryan asked.

"I don't know yet." Jack took one last drag of his cigarette before flinging it away from him, watching as it landed in a puddle of water. "Let's head back to the station and see if anything came in from the evidence. I'm curious what the results will be."

"All right. But let's stop for some breakfast along the way. I'm starving," Ryan complained.

Chapter Five

An hour later, they walked into the precinct. Jack immediately went to Joe Myers' office. He knocked once before entering.

Myers looked up from his task and frowned. "Where's Parks?"

"Making a pit stop. Did anything come in from this morning?" Jack asked without preamble. He took a seat without being asked and stretched his legs out before him.

Myers grunted. "Make yourself at home."

"I am," Jack replied.

Myers sighed. "I have a preliminary report on the girl, but there's nothing really in it," he said, reaching for the manila folder and pushing it in Jack's direction. "Here, take a look."

Jack reached for the folder and opened it, quickly

glancing through the information it contained. "They found traces of marijuana?"

Myers shrugged. "Nothing to get excited about. From what the witnesses at the scene said, they were celebrating that night. They probably had enough of the stuff to get them busted if we had caught them with it, but as it stands now, we just have to put it down to a group of kids blowing off some steam."

"Hardly kids. They were all adults in graduate school. Old enough to know better and to take some responsibility for themselves," Jack responded cynically.

Myers sighed. "It doesn't look like anybody was hurt from it. So they crossed the line of legality. They could have gotten just as high from the alcohol I'm sure was flowing that night."

"I wouldn't say nobody was hurt by it. Lisa Baker was killed."

"But not from overdosing on grass."

Jack shrugged. "Who's to say that she would be dead if she wasn't high? Maybe her reflexes were slowed down. Maybe if she was in total charge of all her faculties, she would still be alive. Maybe she would have been able to get away from her assailant."

"And maybe she would still be dead," Myers returned.

"We'll never know for sure."

Myers laughed. "You're so hard sometimes that it's difficult to think of you as ever being young. I know you're not a saint. I don't understand how you can be so critical of other people."

"Death has a way of doing that to you," Jack replied.

Myers leaned back in his chair and studied him through half-closed eyelids. "The job's getting to you, isn't it?"

Jack let out a sigh and shrugged wearily. "It gets old sometimes, that's all."

Myers nodded. "I know. I feel the same way. If it weren't for my pension, I probably would have called it quits long ago. Life seems to hold very little meaning when you see death on a daily basis."

"I wouldn't say that," Jack denied. "I just get tired of seeing the faces of death. I know it's a natural part of life, but seeing such a careless disregard for it takes its toll."

"Yes, it does. My question to you is, how much of a toll is it taking on you?" Myers asked in all seriousness, as he studied Jack across the expanse of his desk and waited for the answer.

"What do you mean?"

"I mean, you're a good cop, one of the best, but I've seen you take a lot of unnecessary chances lately in solving these cases. So far, it's all been with regards to the law and you've been extremely lucky not to have charges pressed against you. But I would really hate for you to start taking chances with your life."

"I'm not suicidal, if that's what you mean."

Myers shook his head. "It's not. I like you, Jack. I

would hate for you to bite the bullet because you got careless in your quest for solving a case. You have a wife now to think about. You need to take a little more care in how you go about things."

"I'm very careful," Jack asserted. "I'm not quite ready to check out of this life yet."

Myers shook his head, denying Jack's claim. "No, you're not careful. You take things too personally. You make it your mission to put the killers away. It's what makes you a good cop. But, you have to find a balance in life if it's going to be worth living."

Jack laughed, but it held no humor. "Yeah, well, you try telling a victim's family that you can't put everything you have into the case because you have to keep your life balanced."

"That's not what I mean and you know it. You have to take a break from the job."

"It's easier said than done."

"I know," Myers acknowledged gravely. "But for your own sake, you'd better try. Being dedicated is fine. Making it your life's work isn't. It's too intense. No human being can hold up to that type of pressure. You can't save the world. No matter how hard you try."

"That it?" Jack asked, a bored expression on his face.

Myers shot forward in his seat, his brow furrowed in a frown at Jack's cavalier attitude. "No, that's not it. I wasn't going to tell you this, but my meeting with Internal Affairs this morning was about you. About your methods of collecting evidence. About your care-less disregard for the rights of the criminals."

"My disregard for the rights of the criminals! What's that supposed to mean?" Jack ground out.

Myers sighed and ran a shaky hand through his hair. "Apparently, you stepped on several people's toes in your pursuit to solve cases recently. And I have to be honest with you, those people are after your badge."

Jack sat up in his chair, aggression marring his features. "My badge? I solved all of those cases. Nobody walked because of any technicalities. I covered all of the bases."

"Yeah, you did. Afterwards. But if you followed the law to begin with, you wouldn't have to cover all of the bases."

"That's garbage!"

Myers took a deep breath. "Jack," he said in warning.

"No, I don't want to hear it. Everybody I put away was guilty as sin. I know it, you know it, and Internal Affairs knows it. My failure to play it by the book doesn't change that."

"No, it doesn't," Myers acknowledged. "It does, however, cause me a lot of aggravation trying to cover your actions. I'm telling you as a friend, you'd better start watching your step. I can't keep bailing you out."

Jack leaned back in his chair, hearing it creak as it took his full weight. "Is the lecture over?" he asked, his voice full of pent-up aggression.

Myers looked at him for a moment and knew for

now there was nothing else to be said. "Yeah, it's over. Did you come up with anything at the university?" he asked, changing the subject abruptly.

"No. The way they tell it, Lisa Baker was held in the highest of esteem. But there has to be something else there. We just haven't stumbled across it yet," Jack said.

"Stumbled across what?" Ryan asked as he walked into the office and took a seat.

Myers leaned back in his swivel chair and steepled his hands before his mouth. "Jack seems to think that there's something more here than meets the eye. He's not satisfied that nothing has come up yet."

Ryan leaned forward, his hands clasped before him. "To be honest, neither am I. Granted, when there's a death, most people go out of their way to say good things about the deceased, but what we heard today went beyond the ordinary. Nobody can be the way these people are portraying this girl to be."

Jack handed the folder he still held over to Ryan. "Take a look," he invited.

Ryan frowned, but opened the folder and read through the pages. "She did grass."

Jack nodded. "I don't know about you, but from what I heard this morning, the girl never touched a drop of alcohol, never touched drugs, never cursed, and never smoked."

Ryan laughed. "Maybe they'll claim that she held the joint, but she never inhaled."

"That does seem to be the national anthem, doesn't it?" Jack replied with a smirk.

Myers sighed. "I have no idea what you two are talking about, and I don't have time to discuss it right now. I'm late for a meeting. If you don't buy the story you got today, go out and see what else you can dig up."

Jack turned to Ryan. "Let's get the appropriate papers together and head over to her apartment. Maybe something is there that we can tie into this mess."

"Sure. I'll call right now for the search warrant," Ryan replied as he stood and left the office.

Myers looked at Jack, assessing him shrewdly. "Going to play it by the book?" he asked in concern, referring to Jack's penchant for acting first and worrying about the legal system later.

Jack shrugged. "Don't worry about a thing."

"Easier said than done," Myers muttered. "I mean it, Jack. You better start taking some precautions before it's too late. I thought when you got involved with Ashley you would settle down, at least a little bit. How do you think she would feel if something happened to you?"

"Everything's under control."

"Is it?" Myers asked, his voice full of doubt.

"Don't worry about it," Jack said as he stood and walked over to the door. He turned and looked back at Myers. "What about Lisa Baker's family? Did the search turn up anything?"

Myers shook his head. "Her parents died in a plane

crash a couple of years ago. She has no siblings or any other relatives that we can come up with."

"Who's going to make her funeral arrangements?"

Myers shrugged, his facial expression reflecting concern. "I have no idea yet. Nobody came forward volunteering. We're still running some checks, but it looks like we may come up blank on this one."

Jack felt a pang of sympathy. "It's a shame that a life has to end like that. Somehow it's made even worse when you find out that she had no family to care."

Myers nodded. "I agree. I hate this part of the job. Sometimes it's hard not to get emotionally involved."

"I know," Jack said before turning and walking through the door.

Ryan was just hanging up the phone when Jack found him. "It's all set," he told him.

"No problems?" Jack asked as he walked over to the coffeepot and poured himself a cup of the thick brew.

Ryan grimaced. "How can you drink that stuff? You know it's not fresh. It's probably from yesterday morning. I think Myers made it, and you know nobody likes his coffee."

Jack lifted a shoulder carelessly. "It's better than nothing. How long before we can pick up the warrant?"

Ryan looked at his watch. "They said to give them ten minutes. They'll have everything signed by then."

"Myers said she had no family," Jack said.

Ryan looked up, a small grin on his face. "That doesn't mean we're going to take any chances with walking in without a warrant. I swear that sometimes you act like you just want to see what you can get away with without being nailed."

"It makes life interesting."

Ryan laughed. "You have somebody other than yourself to think of now. What would Ashley think if you got caught on something so trivial?"

Jack's eyebrow rose. "I would never hear the end of it. She worries more than anybody I've ever known."

"I know she does," Ryan admitted. "Which is why we're going to play this straight."

Jack shrugged. "Did any of the evidence turn up anything?"

"Nothing concrete, which is about what we suspected."

"What about the background check on the caretaker?"

Ryan reached for an envelope lying on his desk and handed it to Jack. "Take a look."

Jack took the envelope and opened it, reaching inside to remove the small stack of pages. He sat down at his desk and leaned back, kicking his legs out in front of him as he began to read.

"Let me know what you think," Ryan said.

Jack nodded and continued to scan the document. "He did time in a mental institution."

"I know," Ryan replied. "But it also says that he checked himself in due to stress from the job."

"What kind of stress could a caretaker at a cemetery have?"

"I don't know. If I had to work around dead people all day, I would be stressed out."

Jack looked up at him, one eyebrow raised. "I hate to tell you this, Ry, but you do work around dead people all day. In case it's escaped your notice, we work homicide."

Ryan laughed. "You know what I mean. We just see the bodies at the scene or at the morgue. We don't have to live in the same place as them."

Jack shook his head and smirked before continuing with the report. "It says here that his family used to own a string of funeral homes. It would be worth our while to check into it. Maybe this guy has a screw loose somewhere."

"I had a feeling you would say that," Ryan replied, sighing with resignation.

"Good. Then you won't mind if we look into it this afternoon."

"No, I don't mind," Ryan responded as he looked at his watch. "Let's go. The warrant should be ready by the time we get there."

Jack took one final sip of his coffee and put the report back into the envelope. "I'm right behind you."

Chapter Six

Jack and Ryan pulled up to the apartment complex where Lisa Baker had lived. The building itself was all brick, with what appeared to be one main entrance that housed the individual apartments. The outside grounds were mostly poured concrete, with just a border of hedges that should have softened the building's appearance. But the hedges were bare, not yet boasting their spring leaves, making the landscape look barren. Few cars were in the adjacent parking lot. The blacktop was aged and cracked, liberally sprinkled with potholes that could easily flatten a tire. The whole appearance of the complex was one of abandoned isolation.

Across the street was a deserted industrial building, coated with layers of grime so intense that algae was growing along its walls. The windows of the structure were mostly broken, leaving gaping holes that allowed the wind to whistle though. The neighborhood was neglected. It was a place where crime could run rampant if it had a mind to, a place where one could get lost and never be found.

Jack looked around with interest as he brought the car to a complete stop. He parked on the road, choosing not to drive across the gaping holes that liberally sprinkled the blacktop. He cursed as he felt the front wheel of the car sink into the black tar.

"This place should be condemned," he said, his tone full of disgust at the rundown condition of the neighborhood.

Ryan shrugged, but his eyes mirrored the disgust in Jack's voice. "It does look a little worse for wear."

"A little? It's probably rat-infested. I don't think it would pass an inspection with the Board of Health."

"I don't think so either, but I guess kids can't afford much in rent," Ryan replied, trying to find an excuse, any excuse of why someone would choose to live in these conditions. He knew money was a primary concern with anybody regarding where they could live, but he also knew that Lisa Baker could have stayed in the housing located on the campus grounds. If she chose to live here, there had to be a reason. He was very interested in what that reason was going to turn out to be.

Jack shook his head in distaste. "What is it with you and Myers? You speak of Lisa Baker and her group of friends as if they were kids. They're not. They're in their twenties and in graduate school. It's not like they don't know right from wrong."

Ryan looked over at him and frowned. "Hey, Jack, calm down. What is it with you anyway? Ever since the autopsy report came back stating that grass was found in her system, you seem to have set yourself up as judge and jury. What gives?"

Jack rubbed a weary hand over his eyes. "Nothing."

Ryan studied him in silence, trying to gauge the sincerity of the statement without luck. He had never been able to read Jack, not unless Jack wanted him to. Jack was a very private individual, and he guarded his privacy with a frightening tenacity. Ryan sometimes wondered what had happened in his life that he couldn't allow people to get a glimpse of his true self. He didn't know anybody else who had the capacity to withdraw into himself so much so that the outside world couldn't even catch a glimpse of the real man.

Feeling Ryan's eyes on him, Jack turned. "What?"

Ryan shook his head. "Something's bothering you. What is it?"

Jack sighed. "It's nothing. I just can't help but wonder if she had been in full charge of all of her faculties, if she still would have been killed."

"That's something we'll never know."

"I hate not knowing," Jack admitted reluctantly as he switched off the ignition.

Ryan nodded slightly in understanding. "Yeah, me too. Sometimes you wonder if some of the victims would still be alive if they had just used a little common sense. If they had been a little more careful in their actions, a little more cautious in their surroundings."

"Yeah, sometimes you wonder."

"But you have to realize, it's human nature to believe that bad things only happen to other people. Most of us go through life believing that we're invincible, that the atrocities reported on the evening news don't apply to us, that they couldn't happen to us."

"I know," Jack said, acknowledging the truth behind Ryan's words.

"You can't change the world, Jack."

Jack emitted a humorless laugh. "Yeah, so I've been told. Come on. Let's go and check out this place."

Ryan looked at him for a brief moment longer before nodding. "Sure," he replied as he reached for his door handle. Stepping out of the vehicle into the cool spring day, he shaded his eyes against the afternoon glare of the sun that had finally broken through the clouds. "I never expected to see the sun today," he said quietly, glancing around with interest.

"I know what you mean."

"That Jeep over there looks a lot like Ashley's," Ryan said innocently, not expecting any sort of reaction. It was a comment, an observation, nothing more.

Jack stiffened at the words and quickly turned to look where Ryan was motioning. Sure enough, parked across the street was a gleaming black Jeep. Intuition told him that it belonged to his wife. He couldn't believe he had not noticed it sooner. It seemed to exemplify the fact that he was losing his concentration, that he was getting careless.

The conversation Ashley had brought up that morning before he had left for work was burned vividly into his memory. Ashley was too smart to bring up the subject of going back to field reporting unless she had plans to do exactly that. He immediately felt his blood pressure begin to rise at the sight of the vehicle and the knowledge that she was there. "I'll be right back," he said as he quickly crossed the road to where the vehicle was parked.

He looked at the license plate identifying the car as Ashley's, even though he had known it was. Walking to the driver's side, he reached for the door handle and tested it, not surprised when the alarm sounded. Cursing under his breath, he reached for his own keychain that held the alarm control and quickly disengaged it.

He looked around the immediate vicinity, searching for Ashley. He had thought for sure that she would appear once the alarm sounded, but she was nowhere in sight. Concern for her well-being began to gnaw at him. Ashley loved her Jeep, and under normal circumstances, she would have come running as soon as she heard the alarm. The fact that she hadn't made him uneasy. The neighborhood was quiet, too quiet.

Ryan crossed the street, concern etched in his features. "It's Ashley's, isn't it?"

"It's hers."

"What do you think she's doing here? Do you think

there's a problem at home and she decided to track you down?" Ryan asked.

"No, I don't think that's it," Jack said, his tone of voice preoccupied as his eyes continued to scan the area for any sign of Ashley.

"Then why would she be here?"

Jack looked over at him. "This morning, she was talking about going back to reporting."

Ryan looked at him, a shocked expression on his face. "You think that's why she's here?"

Jack reached up to rub the back of his neck as he felt tension begin to build. "Yeah."

"She changed her mind about writing the weekly column? I thought she was excited about it."

"Tom Black asked her to reconsider her decision of moving over to Op-Ed," Jack admitted reluctantly.

"Reconsider her decision? Do you think that's what she's doing?"

"I don't know. I know how much she loves reporting. She thrives on the excitement. I'm not sure how much convincing it would take on his part to get her to change her mind."

Ryan shook his head. "Doesn't she realize that showing up at the crime scenes is dangerous? That it puts her at risk?"

Jack ran a restless hand through his hair. "No. I can't seem to get her to grasp the fact that when she puts herself out there like that, it makes her an easy target for any psychopath watching that wants to get their name in the paper."

Ryan took a deep breath and tried to bring the situation into perspective. "Maybe there's another reason why she's in the area, other than covering this story."

"Like what?"

Ryan thought about it for a moment before shrugging. "I don't know, but I'm sure she'll have a good explanation."

"I hope so," Jack murmured distractedly, his concern for Ashley's safety uppermost in his mind.

"Ashley's too smart to allow herself to deliberately walk into a dangerous situation," Ryan reminded him. "She's not going to take any unnecessary chances with her safety. We just have to stay calm and trust that."

Chapter Seven

They entered the apartment building and were immediately assaulted by the smell of fresh paint.

"At least the interior is in better condition than the exterior," Ryan said in heartfelt relief.

"Yeah. I thought for sure we were going to be walking into another crack house," Jack agreed, his eyes taking in the newspapers that littered the floor near the row of metal mailboxes. They were wrapped and tied, as if they had been delivered and left to be claimed. There was no trash on the floor, no pieces of paper lying about. Both the ashtray and the small waste container had recently been cleaned.

As they walked further into the corridor, they came upon another door that they had to get past in order to access the apartment.

"Which apartment did you say she lived in?" Jack

asked, his eyes roaming around the tight confines of the entry, searching for signs of life. There were no voices—the place was totally silent, as if they were the only two people around. He walked closer to the door that separated the apartments from the foyer, and pushed at it experimentally. The door didn't budge.

Ryan reached into his suit jacket and removed a small black book. He flipped it open and glanced down at the writing. "According to the records, she resided in apartment number one-thirteen."

"That must mean the apartment's on the first floor," Jack stated absently as he continued to examine the lock. There was no latch to maneuver. It needed a key to be opened.

"Yeah. Now all we have to do is find a way to get through that door and into the corridor," Ryan said.

"Any ideas?" Jack asked.

Ryan shook his head. "No."

"We could always break the glass," Jack suggested, his tone of voice suggesting that he was serious.

Ryan sighed and ran a hand through his hair. "I'd like to play this one by the book, even if you don't want to."

Jack looked over at him, a disgusted expression crossing his face. "You must have been a thrill to be around when you were a kid," he complained.

"Why?"

"You like to do everything by the book. I bet you were even a hall monitor in school."

The flush that crossed over Ryan's features had Jack biting back a laugh. "I'm right, aren't I?" Jack asked.

"So? There's nothing wrong with it," Ryan shot back, his voice defensive.

Jack bit the inside of his lip to keep from laughing. "No, of course there isn't anything wrong with it."

"It's one of the reasons I decided to become a cop," Ryan admitted self-consciously, with a slight grin.

"Really?" Jack asked, intrigued despite himself.

"Yeah. I liked the power of telling people what they could do and what they couldn't do."

Jack opened his mouth to reply when the sudden slamming of a door brought his head up. He automatically reached for his gun, pulling it from its holster.

"What is it?" Ryan asked, his hand reaching for his own gun. "Do you see anything?"

Jack shook his head. "No, but I could have sworn that we were alone here."

"You forgot one thing."

"What's that?"

"Ashley's car is outside," Ryan reminded him.

"Believe me, I didn't forget that. I couldn't forget that."

"Maybe Ashley's already inside."

"You think she could have gained access to the apartment when we haven't been able to?" Jack questioned, his brow furrowed in a frown.

"She found access to a lot of places before we did, if you recall. Or at least at the same time we did."

"She is resourceful," Jack granted, his voice betraying a hint of pride.

"That she is."

"So let's go and check it out," Jack said as he moved toward the glass door.

"How? The door's locked. I told you that I wanted to play this straight. You may be willing to take unnecessary chances with your career lately, but I'm a lifer. I want my pension before I'm kicked off the force," Ryan said, his voice rough and guttural.

"Would you just chill out already," Jack grumbled, right before he placed his heavy boot against the lock plate and kicked.

"What are you doing?" Ryan ground out, just as the door swung heavily inward, banging against the wall.

"Gaining access," Jack replied gruffly as he kept his gun pulled and made his way inside, keeping his back to the wall.

"Great," Ryan muttered angrily.

Jack looked over his shoulder to where Ryan still stood. "Well? Are you coming or not?"

Ryan closed his eyes for a brief moment and sighed. "I'm coming," he said, following Jack with his own gun pulled.

"What's the matter?"

"What makes you think there's something wrong?" Ryan asked sarcastically.

"What's the problem, Ryan? We needed to gain access and the door was locked. We have a legal search warrant. As far as I'm concerned, we played this one by the book."

"You know as well as I do that the warrant only

covers her apartment. Not damaging other people's property."

"There's a very good chance that my wife is in this building. If you think that I would be willing to wait until somebody returned to let us in, you're crazy."

"We're not even sure if the noise we heard came from Ashley," Ryan pointed out.

"That's right, we're not. I'm not willing to take the chance that somebody else is in here with her. You know as well as I do that she would do whatever it takes to get a story. If there was a way in here, she found it."

Ryan nodded his head resignedly. "I know. I'm just glad that she's your problem and not mine."

"Let's go and find the apartment," Jack said as he edged his way down the long corridor.

"I'm right behind you."

The apartment was near the end of the hall. Jack reached for the doorknob and turned the handle. "It's locked."

"Check on top of the doorframe. Maybe she left a spare key there," Ryan suggested.

Jack reached up a hand to feel the wood that framed the door. He never did understand what caused people to leave a key in such an obvious place. It was an open invitation to be robbed. He raised his eyebrows as his hand felt a small metal object. He smiled triumphantly as he pulled down a brass key covered with dust. "Pay dirt."

"Told you."

"Yeah, you did. Let's go," Jack said as he inserted

the key into the lock and turned it. He heard the dead-bolt click out of the lock and he turned to Ryan expectantly. "Ready?"

Ryan took position on the opposite side of the door. "Let's do it."

Jack turned the knob and pushed open the door. He stepped inside the doorway, his gun pulled and ready to fire.

They entered the apartment slowly, searching the interior for any movement or sound, anything out of the ordinary.

Jack looked around curiously, noticing that the apartment held few material possessions. The furnishings were sparse, indicating a strict budget. His eyes fell to the red brick fireplace that dominated the room. Hanging from the wooden mantle and around its perimeter were different herbs, tied in bunches and hanging upside down as if to dry.

He was reaching out to touch one of the arrangements when a soft banging sound vibrated through the silent apartment. His eyes immediately searched the room, falling on a closed door. His gun cocked, he motioned to Ryan to follow him as he moved quietly toward the door. His ears were alerted to the slightest noise as he kept his eyes trained on the door.

He reached for the doorknob and slowly turned it, trying not to make a sound. If there was somebody in the apartment with them, he would prefer that he and Ryan maintained the upper hand.

The door opened easily, and he held the side of it

as he eased it open, praying that it wouldn't creak. He moved slowly into the room, all of his senses alert and his adrenaline flowing.

His eyes scanned the interior of the bedroom, immediately focusing on the partially made-up bed and the clothes scattered on the floor. He glanced at the window, noticing it was wide open. A soft breeze was flowing through, blowing on the vertical blinds and causing them to clang.

Ryan immediately put his gun away with a sigh of relief. "It's just the blinds rattling."

Jack moved closer and reached out to part the slats of the blinds. His eyes immediately fell on Ashley's Jeep. It was still parked outside in the same spot. Leaning out the window, he searched the grounds outside, looking left and right for any sign of life. A lone squirrel scurried up the trunk of a tree, but otherwise the place was a ghost town. There wasn't even any traffic traveling the road. The whole scenario was strange. He didn't think there was a place left on Long Island that was so isolated, so far removed from human life in the middle of the afternoon.

"Anything out there?" Ryan asked.

Jack shook his head. "No. The place is deserted."

Ryan shook his head slightly. "There's something strange about the whole setup. It's as if nobody lives in this building. You would think there would be a landlord or superintendent on the premises watching the place."

"I know," Jack said as he left his place by the window and walked over to the double dresser that stood against one of the walls. His eyes scanned the multiple photographs that rested there.

Ryan walked over to join Jack. "She liked pictures," he acknowledged.

"That's an understatement," Jack said as he studied the different photographs, as if searching for an answer.

"What's the matter?" Ryan asked, noticing Jack's focus on one picture in particular.

"What?" Jack asked, as if coming out of a daze.

"What do you see that bothers you? You were studying that picture," Ryan said, reaching out to pick up the photograph that had captured Jack's attention.

"They're all dressed in black," Jack said, motioning to the large group of people in the photo.

"So?"

Jack shrugged. "Nothing. It just struck me as strange."

"Maybe they like the color black."

"Maybe. Or maybe it symbolizes something."

"Like what?" Ryan asked.

"I'm not sure," Jack replied, turning away from the dresser and walking over to the closet.

Ryan put the photograph back down and turned to watch Jack. "There doesn't appear to be anything out of the ordinary here."

"That's a matter of opinion," Jack said as he reached for the handle of the closet. Pulling open the door, he came face to face with his wife.

Chapter Eight

Jack's shock at finding Ashley in the apartment was quickly overshadowed by a sense of relief that she was all right. He automatically reached out to help her from the closet, noticing her torn jeans and white polo shirt smudged with dirt. Her hair was windblown and a streak of soot adorned one cheek. He ran an agitated hand through his hair as all the scenarios of how she might have gotten into the apartment flew through his mind. From the look of her clothes, she had climbed in through the window. He couldn't believe the risk she had taken by entering the apartment. Anybody could have found her, and he briefly closed his eyes as he thought of what could have happened had someone else discovered her.

He debated whether to read her the riot act for breaking and entering. What she did constituted a felony. No gloves covered her hands—her fingerprints were probably all over the place. If collecting evidence from the apartment became necessary, she had just contaminated whatever they would have been able to find. As the repercussions of what she did sunk in, he stared at her silently, trying to come to terms with his conflicting emotions.

Ashley Reeves looked up at her husband's face. She knew she needed to offer him a plausible explanation for her presence. Jack took his job seriously, and he would consider her appearance at a potential crime investigation area a serious transgression of police procedure. "I can explain, Jack," she said softly.

"I'm sure you can," he replied. He looked at her expectantly, curious how she would attempt to justify her presence in the apartment.

Ryan had been standing idly by, watching the exchange between the two. Realizing that they seemed to have forgotten his presence, he stepped forward. "Hi, Ashley," he offered in way of greeting, trying to diffuse some of the tension that was beginning to vibrate through the room.

Ashley looked at Jack for a brief moment longer before turning to Ryan. "Hi," she said with a smile.

"I wish I could say I'm surprised to see you, but that would be a lie. We saw your car outside," Ryan told her offhandedly, almost as if he was discussing the weather.

Ashley sighed at his words. She should have known that her car would be conspicuous if they had gotten there before she had managed to get out. She was angry at herself for her lack of insight. Normally she was more quick-witted, more careful. "I was hoping I would be out of here before the two of you got here," she admitted slowly, not wanting to see or hear the reaction of her husband at her confession, but not willing to make the situation any worse. This was not how she envisioned the start of their married life together. Judging by Jack's facial expression, it wasn't how he envisioned it either.

"You knew we were coming?" Jack asked in disbelief.

"I called the station," she admitted. "Myers said you were going to go and check out something relating to a case you were working on. I put two and two together and came up with four."

"What were you thinking of when you decided to come here?" Jack asked, trying to comprehend the reasoning behind her actions.

"What do you mean?" she asked.

"I mean, you could have run into anybody. What would you have done if it wasn't me who found you? If the killer was the one who found you? Why would you deliberately put yourself in danger like that? And don't tell me the thought of running into somebody didn't cross your mind. I'm quite sure you weren't in the closet taking inventory of the contents."

Ashley heard the concern in his words and shrugged helplessly, unable to deny that she had acted carelessly. "No, you're right. But the fact of the matter is that I didn't think about it until I heard someone in the apartment. And at that point, it was too late to leave. The bedroom doesn't have a balcony. Other than going out the window, the closet was the only other option. Thinking about it now, it probably would have been better to leave through the window. I didn't recognize your voices until you came into the bedroom. If it had been someone else who discovered me, I would have effectively blocked myself in," she said, knowing that she surprised him by her admission.

"Ashley," he began.

She quickly interrupted him. "Jack, if I admit that I made a mistake, could we continue this discussion at home?" she asked, wanting to explain the motivation behind her actions without Ryan as an audience.

Jack looked at her for a long moment before nodding. He wanted to talk to her, but he knew that now wasn't the time. "Yeah, we can talk about this at home."

Ashley offered him a brief smile. "Thank you."

Jack shook his head and sighed. "So tell me, how did you hear about the murder?" he asked.

"Tom Black called me this morning," she said.

"It figures he would somehow be involved," Jack stated.

"What's that supposed to mean?" she asked.

Jack ignored her question. "Why would he tell you about the murder?" he asked, fearing he already knew the answer.

Ashley shifted uncomfortably under his gaze. "He

thought I might be interested in covering the story for him. He said to think of it as one final swan song before I disappear into obscurity."

Jack rolled his eyes at the dramatics behind her words. "I hardly think writing your own column qualifies you for retirement."

"No, but even you have to admit that it lacks a certain amount of excitement," she insisted.

Jack didn't reply to her statement, knowing it wasn't the right time to get into a discussion about her professional future. "I guess you couldn't resist the lure of danger when your editor brought up the subject of the murder. What did he promise you for your agreement to do the story?" he asked, knowing without her saying it that she had agreed.

Ashley shook her head. "Nothing. Tom called me this morning and told me about the body being found at the cemetery. I knew when you left this morning that you had gone to investigate a murder. I checked the police scan, there were no other homicides reported in the area. I thought it wouldn't hurt to check out some leads. Just to see if anything interesting came up."

"You mean you checked with your informant down at the station. Isn't that what happened?"

"I told you what happened," she returned evasively.

"Yeah, you did. Except you forgot one thing. We live in New York. There were multiple homicides last night. The only way you would know which one I was assigned to was for somebody to tell you. Somebody had to tell you. Who's the leak, Ashley?"

Ashley stared at him silently for a moment before shaking her head. "I can't tell you."

"Ashley," Jack said softly, shaking his head in despair.

Ashley reached out to grab his forearm, feeling the muscles tense beneath her touch. "Please listen."

Jack looked at her and sighed. He heard the plea in her voice, in her body language, and he had to fight the urge to comfort her. He could never resist her distress. It was her strongest hold over him. His protective instincts always came out in full force with her. "I'm listening."

Ashley took a deep breath. "When Tom called me this morning and explained what he wanted, my curiosity was piqued," she admitted without apology.

"What did he want you to do?"

"He asked if I would just check out the girl's background to see if there was anything there that was newsworthy. That's all."

"You knew this was the case I was on this morning before you came here?" Jack asked.

"When I called the precinct, Myers confirmed it," she said.

"Yeah, he confirmed it because he's under the impression that you're no longer a reporter. I guarantee you that if he suspected you were after a story, he wouldn't have given you anything."

Ashley shifted uncomfortably, knowing the truth

behind his words. "I'm not sure if I want to stay in reporting, Jack. I mean, the idea of my own column holds a lot of appeal. But I have to admit, I'm not sure if I want to give up reporting permanently. When Tom asked me to check out the girl's background, I thought it would be a good time to see if I could walk away from it."

"Who are you kidding, Ash? You thrive on this kind of stuff. And I haven't a clue as to why."

"Probably the same reason you like being a cop," she returned, not confirming or denying his statement.

Jack shook his head, not replying to her comment. Lately, he didn't like being a cop. It was just who he was. He rubbed the back of his neck wearily. "So what did you come up with?" he asked, changing the subject as he took a step back and looked around the room.

"What did I come up with?" Ashley repeated, somewhat surprised that he was asking for her input.

"Yeah. You went to a lot of trouble to come here, as well as placing yourself at risk. So what did you find out?"

Ashley studied him silently for a moment, trying to determine if he honestly wanted to know her thoughts or if he was just placating her.

"Ash?" he prompted softly when she didn't immediately answer.

The sincerity of his expression convinced her that he was genuinely interested in what she had to say. Flattered that he was asking for her help, she took a deep breath before moving over to the window to look outside. "Did you know this place is practically de-serted?"

"Yeah, we did notice that."

"Do you wonder why? I mean, do you wonder why anybody would choose to live here?"

"What are you getting at?" Jack asked.

"Think about it, Jack. There are no stores around, just a few old houses several blocks away. This block is practically deserted. There are no cars on the street or in the parking lot. There have to be what, maybe twenty apartments in this building, yet they all appear to be empty right now."

"What are you trying to say?"

"I have a theory," she admitted.

"What is it?" Jack asked.

"My theory is that she practiced witchcraft."

Chapter Nine

"**W**itchcraft! Where did you get an idea like that?" Jack demanded, studying her as if she was a specimen under a microscope.

"Don't look at me like that," Ashley replied. "I didn't pull the theory out of thin air."

"Where did you get the idea?" Ryan asked her, his face betraying his skepticism of her words. He looked around the room, but he didn't see anything to attribute to the theory she was trying to sell.

Ashley sighed and reached into the back pocket of her jeans. "I found this," she said, pulling a silver pentacle from her back pocket and holding it up for their inspection.

Jack frowned and reached for the object. It was heavy when he took the weight of it in his hand to study it. "A pentagram?"

Ashley shook her head. "No. It's a pentacle."

Jack looked up. "What's the difference?"

Ashley shrugged. "Actually, they both represent the same thing. When you draw the symbol of the pentacle, it's considered a pentagram. In an object such as this, it's a pentacle."

"This one looks like it's made of silver," Jack said.

"Yes," Ashley replied. "She must have worn it around her neck."

"What makes you say that?" Ryan asked as he came closer to take a look.

Jack handed it to him before turning back to Ashley. "Yeah, what makes you say that?"

Ashley shrugged before moving towards the dresser and opening the top drawer. "There are different chains and cords in here to suspend it from," she replied, motioning towards the vast expanse of the drawer.

Jack took a deep breath and walked closer to where she stood. He looked into the drawer and frowned at the paraphernalia that was nestled inside. He noticed a small brass bell, a black book, a pen, a dagger, and white candles, along with the chains Ashley was referring to. "I see you didn't waste any of your time here," he said, somewhat surprised that she had searched the dresser drawers.

"No, I didn't. You should know by now that I try never to waste any time," she rebuked softly.

Jack reached for the dagger and held it up. "It's a

knife, Ash. It doesn't mean anything. We can't even tie it to the murder."

"Wasn't she cut with a knife?" she asked.

"You have been doing your homework," he replied.

Ashley shrugged. "I'm not saying this was the knife that killed her, just that it proves she was practicing witchcraft."

Ryan shook his head and walked over to where they stood, the pentacle still resting in his hand. "I'm not following you. This doesn't prove anything. The girl was studying anthropology at school. This could all be stuff she had for research purposes," he said, his free hand gesturing to the items in the drawer.

Ashley shook her head and reached for the dagger. "No. This is an Athame," she explained.

"Athame?" Ryan questioned.

"Yes. Technically, it's a knife with a double-edged blade. It's used to focus energy and cast protective circles. Unless you practice the craft, you would have no idea of what it was," Ashley told them as she placed the knife back into the drawer.

"And how exactly do you know what it is?" Jack asked, his forehead creased in a frown.

Ashley waved a careless hand through the air. "I did an article on it a few years back."

"You did more than an article, didn't you?" Jack asked, not sure if he really wanted to know the answer.

Ashley gave a husky laugh. "If you're asking if I joined a coven, the answer is no. If you're asking if I gave the pretense of doing that to get the story, then my answer would be yes," she answered honestly, not expecting much of a reaction to her statement.

Jack rubbed a hand across his eyes. "I'm sorry I asked."

Ashley laughed. "Don't be. They say that honesty in a relationship is always a good thing."

"Right."

"What's this book?" Ryan asked, reaching for the black leather-bound volume.

"Hmm? Let me see it," she answered. Taking the book in her hand, she opened the front cover and glanced through it. After thumbing through the pages, she placed it back into the drawer. "It looks like it's a Book of Shadows."

"A Book of Shadows?" Jack repeated.

"Yes. It's used to keep spells, drawings, notes on different herbs and their healing powers, basically anything you want," she said.

"And the pen?" Ryan asked.

Ashley shrugged. "My guess is that it's the Pen of Art," she replied, as if everybody should know that.

Ryan's shoulders lifted in a shrug. "And?" he asked, his voice full of curiosity at her brief description of the object.

Ashley looked up and smiled. "Sorry. Sometimes I forget that not everybody is familiar with the same things I am. The Pen can only be used to write in the Book of Shadows."

"Okay," Ryan said.

Ashley reached for the small bell and held it up,

swinging it slightly back and forth to start the chimes. "This is used in rituals or ceremonies to summon the Goddess."

"I should have known," Ryan interjected.

"Are you sure you're not letting your imagination run away with you, Ash?" Jack asked, not believing what they were discussing, or the authority that she seemed to have on the subject. He couldn't believe that she had actually attempted to join a witch's coven to get a story. He didn't know why the idea shocked him as much as it did. Once she set her mind on something, she went all the way.

Ashley shook her head and placed the bell back in the drawer before turning to face both men. "No, I think I'm right about this." She reached for the pentacle that Ryan still held in his hand. "Do you want to know what this stands for?" she asked, studying the five-pointed object.

"I do," Ryan said, fascinated despite himself.

Ashley smiled, walking over to the bed to sit down. "This one is made of silver, so it symbolizes Moon energy and psychic powers. If it were gold, it would symbolize Sun energy and strength," she told him before touching the points of the star. "Each of the five angles represents a different element. The lower left-hand corner symbolizes Earth and physical stamina. The lower right-hand corner symbolizes Fire and bravery. The upper right-hand corner symbolizes Water and emotions. The upper left-hand corner symbolizes

Air and intelligence. And the topmost point symbolizes Spirit and spirituality."

"Are we dealing with a satanic cult then?" Ryan asked.

Ashley shook her head. "No. The satanic cults use the pentagram inverted. It's only the media that can't distinguish between what stands for good and what stands for evil," she said offhandedly, before touching the outer rim of the pentacle. "This circle around the star deflects and reflects light, bringing the wearer knowledge, insight, and protection."

"She obviously wasn't wearing her symbol the night she was murdered," Jack said, not believing what he was hearing.

"What's the matter, Jack? Don't you believe that people have the right to worship in their own way and with their own beliefs?" she asked.

"It depends what it is. I don't think anybody has the right to hurt anybody else," he returned as he walked away and moved over to the window.

"People who practice Wicca believe in peace and good will. The religion isn't what the late-night movies portray it as," she insisted.

"Right. And that's why she had a dagger in her drawer," Jack said.

Ashley sighed. "You need to be a little more open-minded. People and their beliefs are different. Things don't always fall into neat little categories."

"I'm well aware of that. But even you can't deny that keeping a lethal-looking knife in one's dresser drawer might be pushing things a bit too far. That's not an ordinary pocket knife."

"No, it's not. But as I said, its true purpose isn't to cause harm," she replied.

"Maybe not, but it's more than capable of doing bodily damage," Jack said.

Ashley nodded, unable to deny his logic. "That's true."

Ryan looked around the room. "As interesting as all these items are, we still haven't found anything substantial to tie to this case."

"Of course we did," Ashley replied.

"What?" Ryan asked.

"I just told you she was practicing witchcraft. That's something to go on," she replied.

"No, Ash, Ryan's right. We don't have anything here to take to the bank. Unless we can prove that her murder was somehow tied into this garbage, we're at ground zero on this," Jack said.

"How can you say that? Maybe there are other witches living in this building. Maybe this is where the entire coven resides," Ashley insisted, beginning to move restlessly around the room as her imagination took flight.

"And maybe you need psychiatric counseling," Jack returned, smiling somewhat to take the sting out of his words.

"We should go and investigate at least," she insisted.

"We?" he returned, his whole body becoming stiff

at her inclusion of herself in the plans. He wanted her out of here, out of harm's way. He didn't believe in this garbage that she was spouting, but he did know there was a murderer still on the loose. And for all he knew, the person could have been close to the victim. He didn't want anybody to see Ashley hanging around the place. He didn't want her tied to this mess any more than she already was.

"Yes, we. As in plural."

"You're not investigating this case with us."

"No, I'm not," she agreed. "I'm investigating this story for my editor."

Jack shook his head. "But not with my help. You already broke the law in coming here. Don't ask me to look the other way while we compound the error. This is official police business, Ashley. And you and I both know you have no business even being here."

"I agree with Jack," Ryan told her. "There's no way we could allow you to stay. There's too much risk. We don't know what or who we're dealing with yet." He turned to Jack. "What do you think, Jack?" Ryan asked as he considered Ashley's theory. Though it seemed far-fetched, he was drawn to the possibility that there might be something in the building to link to the murder.

"About what?"

"Should we check out the other apartments while we're here?" Ryan asked, almost cringing at his own question. They didn't have a search warrant for the other apartments, and they had no business being in any of them.

A small smile touched Jack's lips. "You're willing to break the law? What about your precious search warrants?"

Ryan frowned and rubbed a hand wearily across the back of his neck. "Somebody down at the station owes me a favor. I can call him and have him prepare the paperwork. We should at least be able to check out the basement and storage rooms. If there is something here relating to Ashley's theory, maybe we'll be able to uncover it."

Jack looked at him for a moment before replying, "Go ahead. Make the call." Turning back to Ashley, he asked, "Are you about ready to go?"

Ashley stared at his set features, trying to determine if she could change his mind about letting her stay.

"Okay," Ryan said, returning to the room. "We're all set. They'll have the paperwork signed and sealed when we get back to the station."

"Good," Jack said. He reached for Ashley's hand, not giving her a chance to voice her argument. "Come on. I'll walk you to your car."

Chapter Ten

It was later that evening when Jack could break away from the station and begin the short drive home. He opened the windows of the car, letting the cool evening breeze fan his face. The weather was beginning to warm with the onset of the spring months, and he enjoyed the twilight hour as he made his way home. The sun setting in the west had turned the sky brilliant shades of purple, pink, and orange. It was an awe-inspiring sight. And for just a moment, he had forgotten about the risk that Ashley had taken that afternoon. But only for a moment.

The episode of the afternoon was uppermost in his mind as he flicked on the turn signal at his exit. Taking the service road, he automatically followed the small procession of cars headed in his direction while his mind went over the events that had transpired.

After she had left that afternoon, he had contemplated her actions. He even began to understand them somewhat. He knew what her job meant to her. But he couldn't let go of the fact that she had broken into the victim's apartment to get a story, deliberately putting herself at risk. He couldn't understand her motivation for breaking the law.

He was driving on automatic pilot as he neared his street. Before he knew it, he had turned into his driveway. He parked the car and killed the engine, sitting behind the wheel for a moment to stare at the light burning in the bay window that graced the front of the house. Taking a deep breath, he reached for the door handle and pushed open the door of the car before stepping out onto the driveway. He slammed the door in his wake.

Ashley was sitting on the sofa watching the evening news as she heard the car door close. She looked up as Jack walked into the house and shut the door. "Hi," she offered as a way of greeting, trying to determine if he was still upset about finding her in Lisa's apartment.

Jack pushed himself away from the door and walked further into the living room. "Hi."

"Did you have a good day?" she asked, wishing that he had never discovered her that afternoon. She wanted to turn the clock back a day. She wanted to still be on the beach in Hawaii.

He shrugged carelessly. "It was okay," he said as

he walked past her and into the kitchen. Opening the refrigerator door, he removed a bottle of beer and unscrewed the top. Tilting the bottle to his lips, he took a long drink before lowering it and wiping his mouth with the back of his hand.

Ashley had risen from the sofa as he walked past and now stood in the entryway of the kitchen, watching him. "About today, I know you're upset that I was in Lisa Baker's apartment," she said, searching his face for any sign of softening, anything that would allow her the chance to explain her actions. She wanted to be able to communicate with him openly, without any barriers.

"That's putting it mildly."

"I'm sorry," she said, not knowing what else to say.

"You're sorry?"

"I know it was wrong. There's no excuse for what I did," she admitted.

"I'm glad you realize that."

"I wish you would be fair and let me explain," she told him softly.

"Fair? What is fair, Ashley? Is it fair that I walked in today to a potential crime area and you were there? Is it fair that you broke the law and I had to look the other way? Is it fair that you put your life at risk and expected me to ignore it?"

"Jack, please talk to me," she implored.

"I thought that's what we were doing."

She shook her head at his words. "Talk to me rationally. You're not even trying to understand what motivated me today to go to the apartment."

Jack sighed. "I'm trying to understand. I really am," he assured her. "But you have to realize the risk that you took today. Do you have any idea of what could have happened if someone else had discovered you? You were in a place where you had no business being, regardless of your reasoning. Do you realize that you broke the law? If I had found anyone else in that apartment, I would have arrested them on the spot, no questions asked."

"I know."

"So why did you do it?"

"I just wanted . . ." she began, only to pause when she couldn't find the right words.

"What did you want?" he prompted when it seemed she wasn't going to continue.

Ashley took a deep breath. "I just didn't want to lose myself," she finished with a rush.

Jack shook his head at her words. "I'm not sure what you mean."

"I didn't want to give up who I am. My job has defined me for a long time. It sustained me when I thought there was nothing left that life had to offer."

"Ashley," he began, only to be interrupted.

"Jack, listen to me. Reporting is part of who I am. It's what I did when we met. You knew who I was when we started to go out. You knew who I was when you proposed."

"Yes, I knew. And you knew that I didn't like the

chances you took on your job. You want me to accept you for what you are. Fine. I can do that. But can you accept me for what I am?"

"What?" she asked, shaking her head. "I don't understand what you're trying to say."

"Think about it, Ash. How do you think I would feel if something happened to you? How do you think I would be able to go on? You think I would be able to function with all my wits if you were out chasing a story? Especially the stories that you cover?"

"Your job is a lot more dangerous than mine," she reminded him.

"Yeah, you're right. But ask yourself this. How would you feel if you got the call that I was killed while on a case?"

She flinched at his question, turning pasty white. "Don't even say that jokingly!"

"Who's joking? Ask yourself the question, Ashley, and then magnify your answer by a million, and you'll know how I would feel if I ever got the call on you," he told her simply.

Ashley studied him in silence. When he put his feelings in that perspective, it was hard for her to argue. Getting a call that he was injured or killed while on the job was her worst fear. She couldn't blame him for feeling the same way.

"Ashley?" he prompted in concern as she continued to stare at him silently.

"I love you," she told him softly, sincerely, her eyes beginning to shimmer with unshed tears.

Jack shook his head. Placing the bottle of beer on the counter, he walked over to where she stood. "Don't cry," he begged, reaching out to take her into his arms.

"I'm not crying," she said, just as the tears began to flow.

Jack groaned and held her tighter. "Oh, Ash." He knew he had lost his momentum the moment she started to cry. It was the one thing he couldn't watch. It was the one thing he wouldn't be responsible for. "If you love me, then don't put yourself at risk," he begged.

"Strings?"

"No strings, baby. Just a plea. I can't do my job worrying that you're going to be hurt. You can't expect me to be thinking clearly if I'm wondering where you are and what you're doing. I need to know that you're safe."

Ashley heard the heartfelt emotion behind his words and she hugged him tightly. "When Tom called me this morning, I reacted without thinking. I wouldn't deliberately jeopardize your case," she assured him.

Jack pulled back and reached for his handkerchief. He dried her eyes and stared into their watery depths before nodding. "Okay. I believe you. But that doesn't really explain why you went out of your way to be at the site this afternoon. I know you too well not to realize that you get an adrenaline rush from that kind of thing. It's a dangerous type of addiction."

Ashley nodded, accepting the truth behind his

words. She was addicted to the excitement. She loved the rush she got when she was after a story, taking chances she knew she had no business taking. She sometimes wondered if that was why she really did love her job.

"I could try to quit cold turkey," she offered with a trace of a smile as she tried to bring him out of his dark mood.

"Cold turkey, huh?" he asked, a glimmer of a smile reaching his eyes, even though it didn't touch his mouth.

"I could try."

Jack studied her, noticing the seriousness of her voice and expression that belied her teasing words. He couldn't stay angry with her. He didn't want to stay angry with her.

"I wouldn't want you to get withdrawal symptoms, or anything like that," he told her with a slight smile.

"I would risk it for you," she assured him softly, honestly.

"You would?"

"I would."

"No more rushing in where angels fear to tread?"

"No more," she promised.

"Positive?" he asked, his eyes searching hers as if to search her soul.

"Yes."

Jack smiled tenderly and hugged her to him once again. "Okay."

Ashley felt safe the moment he crushed her to his

broad chest. "I love you," she said softly, needing to reiterate her feelings for him with the words.

Jack hugged her tighter. "I love you too, babe," he whispered against her temple.

"Friends?"

"Yeah, friends," he said right before his lips claimed hers.

Chapter Eleven

The following morning, Jack sat across from Ashley at the breakfast table, reading the newspaper. The weather outside was stormy and rain lashed at the windows, the water running down the pane of glass in sheets.

"It looks awful outside," Ashley remarked, studying the pattern of the water as it cascaded down the bay window. She jumped when the sudden roar of thunder rocked the house, followed by lightning only a second later, illuminating the darkened sky with a blinding intensity.

Jack, noticing her action, lowered the paper and studied her across the table. His eyes mirrored the concern in his voice as he asked, "You okay, babe?"

She fidgeted restlessly for a moment as the lights flickered. "Just a little jumpy," she admitted.

"So I see. Care to tell me why?"

Ashley shrugged her shoulder helplessly. "The storm, I guess," she told him just as the lights cut off.

"Great," Jack said, folding the paper down on the table and getting up. He walked over to the fuse box on the wall and pulled open the small door. He flicked the circuit breaker, cursing under his breath when nothing happened. "It's just a power failure," he told her soothingly as he glanced back at her.

"I know."

"So tell me why you're so agitated this morning. Is yesterday catching up to you?" he asked as he walked over to where she sat and placed his hands on her shoulders. He frowned down at her as she visibly started at his touch. He gently began rubbing the tension out of her shoulders. "Hey, relax. It's only me," he said, just as the thunder roared once again.

Ashley leaned into the strength of his hands and closed her eyes as he massaged her shoulders. She could feel the tension begin to leave her body. "I'm not agitated," she said.

"Could have fooled me," Jack said as his hands began a gentle exploration of her back. He smiled as she practically melted under his touch. Ashley had always loved back rubs.

Ashley opened her eyes and tilted her head back to look up at him. "I love you," she said softly.

Jack leaned down and brushed his lips across hers. "I love you too," he assured her, his hands continuing to work their magic.

She smiled up at him. "You know what I'd really like to do today?"

"What?"

"Spend the day together. Just you and me. No outside distractions."

Jack smiled. "I can't think of anything I'd like better."

"Really?"

Jack nodded. "There's only one problem."

"What's that?"

"We both have to go to work."

"We could play hooky."

"We could, but we won't."

"Why not?"

"Honey, did you forget that we just got back from our honeymoon? I don't think either of our bosses would appreciate it if we called in sick today."

"I know," she said, her voice full of disappointment at the reality check. She blinked in surprise as the lights came back on. "The lights are back on."

"Yeah. So are you going to tell me what has you so wired this morning?" he asked casually, wanting to know what had her so worked up.

Ashley shifted a little as his hand found a particularly sensitive spot. "I don't know. The storm, I guess."

Jack frowned and his hands moved to squeeze her shoulders reassuringly. "I don't remember you being afraid of them before," he remarked idly, trying to read her expression.

"I'm not afraid of storms," she quickly denied. "Just a little edgy."

"That's an understatement," he returned, squeezing her shoulders once again before moving back to his seat.

Ashley sighed, missing the feel of his touch. Her attention was caught by the clock on the microwave that needed to be reset now that the power had come back on. She couldn't explain the restless feeling that had come over her, and he was right when he had mentioned that yesterday's events were catching up with her. But she would never admit it. At least not to him. She rose from the table and walked to the microwave, pressing the panel display to correct the setting. "Do you want more coffee?" she asked, turning to look at Jack.

"You're not going to tell me what has you so spooked?" he asked, his eyes shrewdly assessing her motions.

"It's nothing," she assured him before moving to the stove and lifting the coffeepot. "Do you want a refill?"

Jack reached for his mug, draining the contents in one gulp before holding out the cup. "Please."

Ashley walked over to the table and refilled his mug before topping her own off. "You never did tell me what else you found at the apartment building yesterday," she remarked casually, almost holding her breath as she waited for his response. She wasn't sure how he would take the question, but she was curious to find out if they discovered anything else after she had left.

Jack sighed. "I was wondering when you were going to bring that up."

"Were you?"

"No games, Ash," he warned.

"I'm not playing games," she remarked defensively as she moved back to the table and took a seat.

"Aren't you?" he asked, his voice full of doubt as he reached for his coffee.

"Absolutely not," she assured him. "I'm just curious."

"Haven't you heard that curiosity killed the cat?"

"Who's playing games now?" she countered, her eyes narrowing at his tactics.

Jack lifted a shoulder. "I thought sidetracking you was worth a try."

"You thought wrong."

"Obviously."

"So tell me what you found," she insisted, running a finger around the rim of her coffee cup while she studied him across the small table.

"There's really not much to tell," he said with a shrug as he stood up and stretched his legs. He walked over to the window and looked out at the downpour.

"You didn't find anything?" she asked, rising from the table and walking up behind him. She placed an arm around his waist and began rubbing his back with her other hand.

Jack turned, capturing her in his embrace. "Not much."

"What's not much?"

Jack ran a hand through her hair before tilting her face up to his. "There were some strange things in the basement," he told her reluctantly, his hand absently massaging her scalp.

Ashley melted beneath his ministrations. "What type of things?" she asked, her eyes closing on their own accord as she leaned further into his touch.

Jack smiled at her antics and resisted the urge to grab her to him. "A huge pot of some sort."

Ashley's eyes popped open at his words, and she leaned back from him, her back resting against his forearms as she looked up at him with a frown. "A pot?"

"Yeah."

"What did it look like?"

He lifted a shoulder expressively, his own body tensing at the excitement that was beginning to light her eyes. "I don't know. It looked like the old cauldrons in the B movies."

"Hmm," she murmured reflectively.

Jack looked down at her and traced her lips with his forefinger. "What hmm?"

Ashley looked into his eyes, her own shining. "Do you know what a cauldron stands for?"

Jack groaned. "I'm almost afraid to ask."

"Be serious," she admonished.

"I am."

"Jack," she said in warning.

"Ashley," he mimicked.

"I'm trying to explain something to you. It might shed some light on the case."

Jack expelled his breath in a long drawn-out sigh. He realized that she would give him no peace until she had her say, but he couldn't understand the sudden change that had come over her once they began talking about the case. "Okay, explain," he said, leaning back against the counter and releasing his hold on her waist.

Ashley leaned against the opposite counter. "Well, you probably remember from late night movies and such that the cauldron is a tool of witches."

"Ash, you can't be serious with this stuff," Jack said, not fully believing the depth of knowledge she seemed to have on the subject. He began to wonder just how far she went in her endeavor on the witch story when she was researching it.

"I am totally serious. And stop interrupting."

Jack held out his hands in surrender. "Okay, okay. Continue."

"Yes, well as I was saying, it's a tool that witches use. It's usually made of iron, but only because they don't make them anymore. I'm sure if they did, they would be made of stainless steel."

"Ash," he began in warning.

"Jack, I'm serious."

"I know. That's what scares me," he admitted.

"Anyway," she continued as if he had not interrupted, "the cauldron was where poisons and potions were made. In today's society, it's still used in rituals."

"You have to be kidding," he said in disbelief.

"I'm not."

"So what does that prove?" he asked, leaving the counter and walking back to the table. He took a seat and picked up his mug to finish his coffee.

Ashley shrugged, realizing that he was not sharing her excitement. "Nothing really. It just proves that she was practicing witchcraft."

Jack shook his head. "Sorry, sweetheart. It proves nothing."

She frowned at him and walked over to the table. "But how can you say that?"

"Ashley, what you found proves absolutely nothing. We don't even know if the stuff was actually hers."

"Of course it was," she scoffed.

"There's no 'of course' about it. We have no concrete evidence that it belonged to her."

"But who else would it belong to?" she asked, taking a seat and staring at him across the table.

He shrugged. "It's anybody's guess."

"You know as well as I do that it has to be hers. There's no other explanation for the items to be in her room."

"The woman was studying anthropology. Ryan was right yesterday when he said that the items we found could have been just research for a paper or something," Jack said.

"Doubtful."

He gave her a reluctant smile. "It wouldn't hold up in a court of law and you know it."

"But it's not going to be brought up in court. Her practicing doesn't have any relevance on her murder unless a good defense attorney brings it into evidence. But in order for them to do that, the case would have to somehow be tied to the practice of Wicca."

Jack shook his head in frustration. "I don't understand. After all the trouble you went through investigating her, are you finally admitting that this stuff may have absolutely no relevance to the case?"

She blinked at him. "I never said that her practicing had something to do with the murder," she said slowly, as if testing the theory's flavor.

"No?"

"No, of course not. I just found it interesting that she practiced. That's all."

Jack sighed. "Ashley, don't go claiming she practiced this stuff. We have no evidence. And just in case of the off chance that this stuff we found is related to the murder, I don't want the information leaked."

Ashley looked at him, an expression of hurt crossing her features. "You think I would do anything to jeopardize your case?"

"Not intentionally, no," he told her soothingly.

"I would never do it unintentionally either," she assured him.

"Ashley," he began just as the phone rang. He stood up from the chair and walked over to the phone mounted on the wall.

Ashley watched him as he spoke, trying to decipher the gist of the conversation, but his voice was too low, and the person on the other end of the phone was doing most of the talking. She looked at him expectantly as he hung up.

Jack looked over at her, his features grim. "That was Ryan. There's been another murder."

Chapter Twelve

"Another murder?" Ashley repeated.

Jack rubbed a weary hand across the back of his neck, feeling the tension begin to build. "Yeah."

"Where?"

"Near the old Methodist church," he admitted grudgingly, watching her expression and waiting for her to jump on the bandwagon about going with him to the scene. He wasn't up to another confrontation on the subject. They had talked into the early morning hours, and he felt fairly confident that she understood his concern about her covering this story. However, one look at her face had him doubting the theory. He mentally braced himself for another argument.

Ashley's eyes widened slightly. "There's a cemetery right next door to the church grounds, isn't there?"

"Yeah, there is. The cemetery belongs to the church.

It's no longer used though. I don't think anybody has been buried there since the late 1800s."

"Until today," she interjected.

"Until today," he confirmed. He moved toward the open doorway. "I'm going to go and finish getting dressed. I told Ryan I would meet him at the scene."

Ashley rose from the table and followed him into the bedroom. She stood in the doorway while he took some clothes out of the closet. "I'd like to come with you," she said softly. She knew he wouldn't be happy with her request.

Jack's head shot up and he glared at her. "You have to be kidding me," he returned in disbelief.

Ashley lifted one shoulder and left the doorway to cross over to the bed. She sat down on the edge of it. "I'm not," she told him honestly.

Jack shook his head. "I thought we had all of this settled."

"I just want to finish covering this one story. I can't explain why. I wish I could," she said.

"What's so special about this case?"

She shrugged. "I'm not quite sure. It fascinates me for some reason."

Jack shook his head and walked over to where she sat. He absently ran a hand down her hair. "Don't ask me this, Ash."

She leaned into his touch and looked up into his grim features. She wished she could explain to him the hold this case had over her. She wished she could explain it to herself. "Please, Jack."

"No," he said with a sigh, releasing her hair and walking into the bathroom. He kept the door open while he stepped into the shower.

Ashley heard the water running and leaned back in the bed, inching up until she rested against the pillows. She watched the steam begin to fill the small enclosure and fog up the mirror. She had to find a way to convince him that it was safe for her to cover this assignment, that he had nothing to worry about.

Ten minutes passed before Jack emerged from the bathroom, a towel slung around his neck. He had already put on his slacks and was buckling the belt. Feeling her eyes on him, he turned to stare at her. "No," he said, answering the unspoken question.

"But why? What harm could it possibly do?"

"What harm?" he asked in disbelief.

"Yes. Tell me what harm."

"How about getting yourself killed? Is that reason enough for my wanting to keep you safe?"

Ashley scoffed. "Nothing is going to happen. I've been covering the same sort of story for years, and nothing has ever happened," she reminded him.

Jack took the towel from his neck and quickly dried his hair before going back into the bathroom to run a comb through it. "I'm not going to let you come with me to a crime scene."

"But I might be able to help," she offered.

Jack shook his head. "I don't need your help."

"But what if it is related to witchcraft?"

"Then I'll solve it on my own."

Ashley sat on the edge of the bed and listened as he used the electric razor. More than anything, she wanted to go with him, but she didn't want to start a war over it. She waited until he came back out.

Jack took one look at her face and sighed. "The matter is closed," he told her decisively as he stood at the mirror and put on his tie.

Ashley stayed on the bed, not saying anything. There was nothing to say that would help the matter.

Jack left the mirror and grabbed his suit jacket. Walking over to the bed, he placed a fleeting kiss on her forehead. "Try and stay out of trouble," he begged.

Ashley didn't say anything. She just watched as he walked out the door.

Thirty minutes later, Jack was entering the gates of the cemetery. The chain link fence that protected the property was old and rusty, the tombstones that lined the grass thin and old. The stones had begun to fall due to age and lack of foundation, giving the cemetery a neglected appearance.

He followed the road to where the flashing lights of the patrol car beckoned. Parking the car, he opened the door, hunching his shoulders against the still falling rain as he made his way to a small group of officers.

Ryan looked up as he approached. "It's about time you got here," he remarked.

"I left the house shortly after you called," Jack replied, walking over to the body that was draped in a sheet. Going down on his haunches, he reached for the edge of the sheet and slowly pulled it back.

"Same M.O.," Ryan said.

"Yeah."

Ryan looked back to the car. "Where's Ashley?"

Jack let the sheet fall back into place and stood up. "What?"

"Ashley. Where is she?" Ryan asked, his eyes scanning the vicinity by the car.

"At home, I hope."

"She couldn't talk you into letting her come?" Ryan asked, a slight smile hovering around his mouth.

Jack glared at him. "Just drop it already."

"Okay, okay, don't get worked up."

"Tell me, did they find any new evidence on this scene?" Jack asked, his hair falling damply around his face from the steadily falling rain. The uniformed officers all had rain jackets on, the hoods concealing their heads, but he could never stand wearing the things.

"Actually," Ryan said, "I think we got lucky on this one."

"Lucky? How?"

Ryan smiled and reached for the black bag that rested by his feet. Undoing the clasp, he removed a clear plastic bag from within. "What do you think?"

Jack took the bag from Ryan's grasp and whistled.

"Look familiar?" Ryan asked.

"Ashley called this what? An Athame?" Jack asked,

turning the bag over and studying the double-edged knife within the clear protective covering.

"Something like that."

"There doesn't look like there's any blood on the blade," Jack said, studying the instrument.

Ryan nodded. "Yeah, I noticed."

Jack looked at him and handed back the bag. "It may not be the murder weapon."

"I know. Unless they wiped the blade clean. Forensics will have to do a couple of tests before we can rule it out entirely."

"When can they get the results back?"

Ryan handed the evidence to one of the technicians loading up a van. "We should know by later this afternoon. The coroner should be able to tell us if the cut to the throat could have been done by that blade."

"I don't know. Something just doesn't add up here," Jack said, reaching for his cigarettes and shaking one out of the pack. He immediately offered one to Ryan.

Ryan accepted the cigarette and lighter. "You're thinking the whole thing is too obvious, aren't you?"

"Something like that," Jack admitted. "What about you?"

Ryan shrugged. "I had thought along the same lines. It's just too convenient of a setup."

"Especially if somebody saw us at the apartment complex yesterday."

Ryan nodded. "I know."

"Did the report come back on the caretaker yet?" Jack asked, taking a deep drag on his cigarette.

"It came back clean," Ryan said.

"Nothing?"

"Nothing. The report was just a shot in the dark anyway. The people we interviewed yesterday after leaving the apartment complex didn't reveal anything noteworthy."

"I know. Still, I was hoping we would begin to put together some pieces of this puzzle. I thought for sure that there would have been at least one skeleton lurking somewhere."

Ryan shrugged. "If there is, we haven't been able to uncover it. It's not listed in any records anyway."

Jack looked around the surrounding area. "It doesn't look like they were able to uncover much else around here," he said, his eyes scanning the property. An old shed stood off to the side. The doors were open and a couple of technicians were snooping around, but it didn't look like they had found anything so far.

"No," Ryan agreed. "There's not even a caretaker for the grounds. The cemetery's not used anymore, the property is managed by the church. And that's locked up tighter than a tomb," he said, gesturing to the heavy padlock that graced the heavy wooden double doors.

Jack nodded. "Maybe it's only used on Sundays."

"Maybe."

"It's strange that there's no housing for the pastor on the property. I thought that there was always a house set aside for them."

Ryan shrugged. "Times are changing. Maybe they

didn't have the money to build anything. And then there's the area."

"What about it?"

Ryan lifted one shoulder. "It's not the nicest of neighborhoods."

Jack looked around. "There are worse."

"True, but it's never a good sign when a church has to use a padlock to keep criminals or trespassers out."

"Well, as you said, the times are changing. I just wish I could figure out the relevance to leaving the body in the cemetery."

"I have to admit, that baffles me also," Ryan replied.

"It has to mean something," Jack insisted.

"Yeah, but what?"

"I don't know."

"Ashley seemed to know a lot on the subject yesterday. Do you think she would have any ideas?" Ryan asked slowly, almost afraid to broach that particular subject.

Jack looked at him. "You don't honestly expect me to ask her, do you?" he asked in disbelief.

"It was just a thought."

"Forget it."

Chapter Thirteen

It was a couple of hours later before the crime scene technicians left. The rain had stopped and Jack watched the last taillight head out of the gates.

"So what do we do now?" Ryan asked, his eyes scanning the cemetery grounds. Only the old fencing offering any kind of protection; it seemed easy enough for somebody to scale the top of the fence and make their way in. But something just didn't add up. The gate had an old rusted padlock on it when the first patrol car had arrived. The officers had to physically cut the chain away from the gate; the keyhole had been closed with a wad of gum. The cemetery had a definitive air of abandonment, the grass dead and bare in most areas, with only weeds gracing the sacred grounds. The place looked as if it had been long forgotten other than the local kids using it as a hangout. As Ryan glanced around, a frown marred his features.

Jack looked over at him, a knowing look on his face. "You're wondering how the killer got the body into the cemetery grounds if the gate was locked, aren't you?"

Ryan shrugged. "Yeah."

Jack nodded. "There might be another way into this place. There seems to be an awful lot of kids that find their way in here to hang out. Maybe there's another entrance."

Ryan shook his head doubtfully. "The kids that found the body today admitted that they climbed over the fence to gain access. That they always climb over the fence. If there was another way in here, don't you think that they would know about it?"

"Maybe, maybe not. They weren't trying to transport dead weight over the fence whenever they made their way over."

"So what do you suggest we do?" Ryan asked, his eyes searching the grounds, looking for any clue that could shed some light on how the killer had brought the body in.

Jack lifted one shoulder expressively and ran a hand over his face. "Let's check out the perimeters of the property. There has to be another way into this place. Maybe we'll luck out and find it."

"You don't think that the killer threw the body over

the fence?" Ryan asked, as his mind raced over possibilities.

Jack looked over at him in disbelief. "You have to be kidding me. The woman that the coroner just took away was no lightweight. Whoever our killer is would have to be superhuman to get that body over that railing," he said, motioning to the top of the fence.

"So what do you suggest we do?" Ryan asked.

"Search the grounds," Jack replied. "It's the only way to be sure that there's not another way in and out."

"And if there is?"

"If there is what? Another way in?"

Ryan nodded. "Yeah. It wouldn't necessarily prove anything."

"No," Jack agreed. "It wouldn't necessarily prove anything. But it may shed some more light on this case. The two murders have too much similarity to be a copycat case."

"Copycat?" Ryan repeated. "To be honest, I didn't even think of that angle."

"It crossed my mind, but only briefly. There wasn't enough of a write-up in the paper for someone to know the ins and outs of the first murder. Not unless they were on the scene before we were."

"Still, it's an interesting theory."

Jack smiled. "But not a possibility."

"Thank God. Could you imagine trying to solve both cases? We would be up to our eyes in paperwork."

"Mm."

"So which direction did you want to search?" Ryan asked.

"I'll go left, you take the right. We'll meet back here when we're through."

"Right," Ryan said, before heading off to his right.

Jack watched him leave before turning away with a sigh. He briefly wondered what Ashley was up to. He didn't entirely trust her to keep away from the story— he knew her too well. Hoping that she would stay away, he headed off to investigate the perimeter of the fence.

As he walked closer to the fence's edge, he noticed the tombstones that were leaning towards the ground. The few graves that had crypt slabs above the ground were faded with age, the marble beginning to separate, giving a brief glimpse into the dark interiors of the tombs.

As he came closer to one crypt, he slowed to a stop, studying the stone and the grounds surrounding it. The grass held an indentation, the dirt mucked up slightly, indicating a recent disturbance. Bending down, Jack reached for the dirt and ran a hand experimentally over it. He was somewhat surprised to find the dirt loose, while the rest of the area was firmly packed. Looking at the concrete slab that rested on the earth, he saw a small opening obscured by shadows.

Going down on his knees, he reached for the cold slab and pushed. Satisfaction rushed through him as the marble easily moved, revealing a dark cavern. He wasted no time levering himself into the dark abyss.

Jack grunted as he fell onto the ground. Rising to his feet, he quickly dusted himself off and reached for the penlight that he always carried. He aimed it around the dark hole while reaching for his handkerchief to cover his mouth and nose. The air in the hole was stagnant and musty, practically choking him. Jack frowned as he realized he was in the catacombs of the cemetery.

He followed the dark path, the small flashlight the only source of light as he made his way through the tunnel. He curiously looked around the small pathway, but there was nothing out of the ordinary that caught his attention. As he followed the winding path, he was forced to a stop by a small staircase.

Putting the flashlight between his teeth to hold the stream of light steady, he reached for the trap door positioned above the stairs. His hands resting on the rough wood, he felt a few splinters enter his skin as he pushed his weight against the door, grunting with satisfaction as it gave way.

The door fell open with a bang as dust rose and filled the air. Jack pushed himself up through the opening, using his hands for leverage, the flashlight still clamped between his teeth. He grunted with satisfaction as he pulled himself through to the floor above.

He sat there for a moment while he shone the flashlight around the dim interior of the room, realizing with the sight of stained glass windows that he was in the church. There was no sound and no light except for the dim color given by the stained glass.

As Jack walked through the nave, he was surprised at the church's air of neglect. It looked as if it hadn't been used in years. The dust cloth that covered the pulpit was gray with grime, and the air was stagnant, as if fresh air had not made its way inside in a long time. He searched the wall for a light switch and made his way over to the far side of the room when he spotted one. Flicking the switch, he was mildly surprised when the lights flickered on. He hadn't expected that. From the air of abandonment that surrounded the church, he would have thought that the electricity would have been disconnected.

The light that illuminated the building had Jack blinking several times as his eyes tried to adjust to the sudden brightness. He looked around with interest, noticing the cobwebs that covered the walls, ceiling, and floors. Most of the items in the church were covered in a thick blanket of dust. Slight scurrying sounds reached his ears, a sure indication that either mice or rats had made themselves at home.

His eyes continued to scan the building. Curiosity gripped him as he noticed a pristine white cloth on the altar. It stood out simply because it was so clean, such a pure white. Walking up to the altar, he reached for the white sheet that covered it and quickly pulled it away from the table.

The sheet fell silently to the floor as Jack caught a glimpse of the altar. It was a gray marble, nothing shocking or even out of the ordinary. But what was on the top of it was startling. It was a pentagram.

"Jack?" a voice yelled, the sound echoing through the old walls of the church.

Jack turned toward the sound, realizing it was coming from the wooden door on the floor. He left the altar and walked over to the opening. "In here, Ryan," he yelled back.

"In where?" Ryan asked, his voice becoming stronger as he neared the spot where Jack stood.

Jack saw him as he neared the staircase. "Right here."

Ryan looked up, a startled expression crossing his features as he spotted Jack. "This place gives me the creeps," he said with a shudder.

"Wait until you see what I found," Jack warned.

"What?"

"Come on up and you'll see."

"I'm almost afraid to see," Ryan replied as he hoisted himself into the church.

"How did you know where to find me?" Jack asked, watching as Ryan stood and dusted himself off.

"I didn't. I was looking for you when I saw the opening at the crypt. I took a guess that you would go in and see what you could find," he said, rolling his eyes upwards.

Jack laughed. "You would have done the same thing."

"I would not," Ryan replied emphatically.

"Yes, you would. As a matter of fact, you just did," Jack pointed out.

Ryan opened his mouth to reply and quickly closed it. "Temporary insanity."

Jack looked at him and shook his head. "Right."

Ryan shrugged. "So show me what you found."

"Come this way."

"I have to tell you, Jack. You could have knocked me over when I saw the opening of that crypt. I didn't think that this place would have a catacomb."

"Yeah, I was a little surprised too. But looking at the interior of the church, other than the front door, that seems to be the only way out."

Ryan looked around with interest. "It doesn't look like this church is used anymore."

"Guess again."

Ryan shot him a sharp look. "What do you mean? The place is covered in cobwebs and dust. You can't tell me that they still hold church services here anymore."

"I think they hold some type of services here. I'm not quite sure what the faith is though."

"Would you stop talking in riddles and tell me what you mean?" Ryan demanded, running a restless hand through his hair.

Jack motioned with his chin to the altar. "Take a look for yourself," he invited.

Ryan frowned and slowly walked towards the altar. His eyes fell onto the sheet that rested on the floor. "Spring cleaning?"

Jack shook his head at the weak joke. "Just go and take a look."

Ryan shrugged. "I'm going. I'm going," he said, walking closer to the altar, his steps slowing as he neared it. His eyes widened once he caught sight of the pentagram, which was painted on the top. "Sweet mother of God."

"Those were my sentiments," Jack replied.

Ryan walked closer and studied the painting. "You think that a cult worships here?"

"Do you have another idea?"

Ryan ran a hand over his eyes as if to wipe out the picture. "I never expected anything like this."

"I know."

"This kind of ties the murders to Ashley's theory. You do realize that, don't you?"

Jack ran a weary hand over the back of his neck, feeling the muscles begin to tense as usual. "I am aware of that fact."

"Did you find anything else?" Ryan asked, beginning to search the surrounding area.

"No. I really didn't get a chance to do much of a search once I saw that. You got here right after."

Ryan stood from his crouched position by the altar. He held a small goblet.

Jack noticed the silver cup and walked over to where Ryan stood. "What did you find?"

Ryan held up the object. "I don't know if it belongs to the church or to the cult," he admitted.

"Is anything in it?"

Ryan ran the tip of his finger around the inside of the cup. "It feels like some sort of oil."

"Oil?"

"Yeah. Do you know what I think we should do?"

Jack glanced at him warily. "What?"

"Ask Ashley if she knows what this means."

"I was afraid you would say that."

Chapter Fourteen

Two hours later, Jack found himself outside the building that housed his wife's office. He couldn't believe that he had let Ryan convince him to get Ashley involved. He had argued with Ryan that they didn't need her to find out what the items in the church meant. That they could go to any store that specialized in the occult and get the same information and maybe more. But he was unable to convince Ryan to go that route. Ryan was too superstitious. He wouldn't set foot in one of those stores unless he absolutely had to. His reasoning was that since Ashley seemed so familiar with what they had found at the apartment complex, there was no reason why they couldn't ask her what the items at the altar meant. Jack normally would have agreed with him. Except that these weren't normal circumstances. This time they were dealing with his wife.

Jack entered the building and immediately went to Ashley's office, wanting to catch her before she left for lunch. He hadn't called her to let her know he would be coming, and he hoped that she hadn't made other plans. He was slightly disconcerted to find her desk empty, but the secretary informed him that Ashley was in the cafeteria, and pointed him in the right direction.

Ashley was in deep conversation with Tom Black when Jack came through the doorway. She looked up in surprise at his entrance. "Jack!"

Jack looked at her for a long moment before inclining his head briefly to Black. He walked across the room to the chair that Ashley occupied. "I need to speak with you," he told her.

Tom Black stood at Jack's entrance, somewhat surprised by his appearance. He quickly recovered and held out his hand. He cleared his throat slightly as he said, "Jack, what a surprise. It's nice to see you again. We didn't expect you."

Jack looked at the extended hand before reaching out to shake it. "I apologize for the interruption, but I need to speak with Ashley."

"Of course," Tom said.

Ashley shook her head slightly, trying to gather her thoughts. "Talk to me?"

Jack extended a hand to her. "Yes. Do you have a moment?"

"Did something happen?" she asked, trying to determine why he found it necessary to track her down.

"No," he assured her, his facial expression softening as he looked at her. "I just need to talk to you. Alone."

Ashley's curiosity was piqued and she turned to look at Tom with an apologetic smile. "Can I call you later?"

"Of course," Black assured her as he began to walk away from the table.

"What's wrong?" she asked the moment Black was out of sight. She glanced briefly at her watch. It was rare for Jack to come to her office during working hours. He was usually tied up with police business. She knew he had to have a good reason to seek her out.

"Let's go for a walk," Jack said, reaching for her hand.

"Is everything all right?" she asked as she let him lead her from the room.

"What were you discussing with Black?" he asked, effectively sidestepping her question. He needed to know if she was going to go through with covering the murder investigation.

Ashley smiled at his question. "Relax. My meeting with Tom was perfectly innocent. I was explaining to him my reasons for not continuing with the story."

Jack stopped dead in his tracks, pulling her to a stop beside him. "Really?" he asked, disbelief in his tone. He stared at her intensely, trying to read from her expression if she was telling the truth.

"Yes, really," she replied. "So what's your excuse for being here?"

Jack hesitated, suddenly reluctant to tell her his true reason in seeking her out. He had the sudden suspicion that once he asked for her help, she would jump back on the bandwagon about investigating the story. He knew it wouldn't be in an effort to aggravate him, but rather because she would be unable to help herself. He didn't blame her for it really, but he wouldn't be able to do his job if he was constantly worrying about her and her whereabouts. His hesitation had Ashley studying him curiously.

"Jack?"

Jack looked at her for a brief moment longer. "You know there was another murder."

"So?"

"So, you also know it was by the old Methodist church."

"I know."

Jack sighed inwardly and ran an agitated hand across the back of his neck as he tried to relieve the mounting tension. Asking her for help went against every principle he possessed, but he knew it was the logical thing to do. Ryan was right. She did seem to know the answers with regards to the occult. When you combined that with her knowledge of the area, she was the reasonable choice to seek answers from. He knew that, but he didn't like it. He studied her silently for a moment before asking, "Do you know if the church is used anymore?"

"Used? In what way?"

"For services."

Ashley bit her lip as she thought seriously about his question. She knew he had a reason for asking it; he wasn't the type to talk just to hear his own voice. "I don't think so," she said after a while, as she tried to recall any stories about the church closing.

"That's what I was afraid of."

"Afraid of?" she repeated. "Why?"

"After the coroner took the body away this morning, Ryan and I started to take a look around the grounds. I found an entrance to a catacomb that leads to the inside of the church."

Ashley's eyes widened at that bit of information as she became fascinated with what he was telling her. She was almost envious of him at that moment. She would have loved to explore something like that. "Really? What was it like?" she asked, excitement beginning to shine in her eyes.

Jack shook his head, a glimmer of a smile touching his mouth as he studied her expression. "Forget it, Ashley. I'm not taking you there to see it."

"Why not?"

"Because it could be dangerous."

"How?"

Jack expelled a long breath and ran an agitated hand through his hair. He hesitated before saying the words. "Because I think some type of cult is using the place."

"A cult?"

"Yeah."

"Really?"

Jack cringed inwardly at the tinge of excitement in her voice. "Don't get carried away."

"What's that remark supposed to mean?" she asked.

"Nothing. Just that you usually thrive on this type of stuff."

"Well, it is exciting. Even you have to admit that."

"Sorry, babe. It's not my type of thing. I don't find it the least bit exciting," he told her.

"Well, I do," she admitted without apology.

"I know," he said, his voice full of resignation.

"So what do you need my help with? Other than finding out if I had heard anything about the church being closed."

"I wanted you to take a look at the items we found at the altar. Maybe you can identify the meaning of some of them."

"What makes you say that?"

Jack shrugged. "You're the one who admitted to joining a witches' coven to get a story."

Ashley studied him for a moment before saying, "That's true."

"So?"

"All right. Let's go and take a look. Maybe we'll be able to find something."

"I was hoping you would say that."

She laughed. "Don't lie."

"I'm not," he assured her.

"Yes, you are. There's no way I can believe that you were hoping that I would get involved in this story," she told him, her voice assuring him that she knew exactly what it cost him to ask for her assistance. She knew he wouldn't ask her if he had a better idea how to get the information.

Jack shrugged without apology. "You can't blame me on that."

"My guess is that it was Ryan who initiated my helping out, wasn't it?"

"Does it matter?" he asked.

Ashley lifted a shoulder. "Not really. I can't deny that I want to see what you found."

"I didn't think you would deny it. You're too honest for that."

"Thank you, I think."

"Don't worry. It was a compliment."

"However backhanded."

"Yeah, well . . ."

"Relax, Jack. I know what it cost you to ask for my help. I'm not going to start arguing with you about covering this story. I meant it when I said that I told Tom I was through with reporting on the police beat."

"Yeah, but for how long?" Jack murmured under his breath as they walked outside.

Chapter Fifteen

Jack was waiting beside his car outside the cemetery grounds for Ashley. They had decided to drive to the cemetery separately so that he wouldn't have to give her a lift back to her office. Now he paced impatiently as he waited for her to show up. He had lost her in the traffic several stoplights back.

Glancing at his watch, he reached for his cigarettes and shook one out. He cupped his hand around his lighter as he lit the tip and took a deep drag off the filter while he waited for his wife to show up. It was almost five minutes since he had arrived. He couldn't help but wonder where Ashley was.

As he looked down the narrow road that led to the cemetery, he felt a wave of relief wash over him as he spotted the black Jeep. The gleaming chrome of the fender glistened in the afternoon light as she pulled the car parallel to his. He watched as she automatically checked her features in the rearview mirror before opening her door and stepping out to the dirt below.

"It's about time you got here," he told her gruffly, his eyes automatically scanning her face ensuring himself that she was okay.

Ashley smiled. "Missed me?"

A wave of tenderness swept over him at her words. "I always miss you when we're not together," he told her honestly. "Is everything all right?"

"What do you mean?"

"It took you awhile to get here. Where did you disappear to?"

"I seemed to hit every stoplight."

He grunted. "No problems?"

"Other than getting stuck every few blocks?"

"Don't be cute."

"Relax, Jack."

Jack didn't answer. He turned and looked through the fence. "Ryan was supposed to be here waiting for us."

Ashley walked over to him and lightly ran her hand across his back. "Hey, relax. Why so uptight?"

Jack turned at her touch and caught her in his arms. He hugged her tightly to his chest before resting his forehead against hers. "I don't like involving you in this," he admitted.

"You're not involving me in anything," she assured him.

"I am."

"No. I'm just helping out. I promised you that I would stay out of this. I meant it."

Jack stared into her eyes and was about to say something when a voice shouted across to them. He quickly turned and noticed Ryan standing by the tomb that led to the catacomb.

"There's Ryan," he murmured.

"Yeah."

"It looks like you may get your wish," Jack said as he released her and stepped back.

"What do you mean?"

"The church is still locked. I guess we're going through the catacomb."

"Why not cut the lock?" she asked, although she was glad she would get to see the catacomb.

Jack shrugged. "We don't want to take the risk of tipping somebody off. This way, they won't know for sure if we know about the place. The church was locked tighter than a drum. We run less risk of being conspicuous this way."

"You don't think they would guess you would get into the church to investigate?" she asked.

"Depends on the stability of the person. Anyway, why are you complaining? I thought you would be thrilled at the opportunity of going underground. That was the impression you gave back at the newspaper, anyway," he reminded her.

"Oh, I am. Believe me, I am. I just thought it was a little strange that you didn't cut the lock already. I would have expected it after the body was discovered in the cemetery."

"We probably would have if we didn't find the other way in. But I don't think the killer expected us to cut the lock. The murder was staged so that it appeared as if the body was dumped."

"Ah, Jack. You do have a way with words."

"What do you mean?" he asked.

"The way you said the body was dumped. It was sheer poetry."

"We can't all be writers, Ash."

"Well, don't worry. Just say the word and I'll write a story that will flush the killer out."

"No!"

"Calm down, calm down. I'll only do it if you want me to. I wasn't making a statement of intent," she assured him.

"Good."

"Relax already, would you? We'd better go and see Ryan. He looks like he's getting a little agitated."

"Ryan's always agitated in cemeteries."

"I wonder why?"

Jack shrugged. "I don't know and I never thought to ask. Probably a carryover from his childhood."

"It might be interesting to find out," she mused.

Jack shot her a knowing look. "Yeah, it might be, but we're not going to ask."

"I was just thinking aloud," she quickly defended herself.

"Uh huh."

"Ah, Jack, chill out already."

"I will. Just as soon as you start talking some sense."

Ashley sighed. "Let's go and meet Ryan."

"Good idea."

Ryan stood with his hands in his pockets, rocking on his heels as they walked over to him. He looked at them curiously, wondering if he had managed to start a mini war over his suggestion of getting Ashley to help them. He hoped not.

"It's about time you two got here," he said in way of greeting as they approached.

"Sorry. It took me a while to find Ashley," Jack said.

"Hello, Ryan," Ashley murmured.

"Hi, Ashley."

"Jack told me about what you found. I can't wait to see it," she assured him.

Ryan nodded. "Well I hope you don't have an aversion to dark, damp places. I didn't see any bodies in the tunnel, but then I'm not quite sure why it's in existence."

"I'm sure it will be fascinating."

"You would feel that way," Jack murmured.

Ashley ignored the comment. "Shall we go?" she asked, her voice laced with excitement.

Jack shook his head. "Ryan, why don't you lead the way?"

"Okay."

The three of them entered the tunnel in succession, Ryan leading the way and Jack bringing up the rear.

"Somehow I thought it would be different," Ashley remarked as she followed Ryan through the tunnel. Other than it being dark and narrow, there was nothing extraordinary about it.

"Did you?" Ryan asked.

"Mm. I guess I've been watching too many late-night horror movies," she said jokingly.

"The only interesting thing about this tunnel is that it exists," Ryan said, stopping once they reached the small door that led to the church. He handed his flash-light to Ashley then reached up with both hands and pushed. The door fell back with a bang, a cloud of dust rising and swirling in the air.

"Watch your step, Ashley," Ryan said as he quickly pulled himself through the opening and held out a hand to assist her.

Jack waited until she cleared the floor before quickly joining them in the church. He immediately turned to Ashley. "Are you okay?" he asked, his eyes sweeping over her.

Ashley nodded and quickly dusted herself off. "I'm fine."

"Good," he said before turning and leading the way to the altar.

Ashley followed, but at a much slower pace. Her eyes were busy scanning the interior of the church. "Are you sure that this place is being used by a cult?" she asked, noting the thick layer of dust that coated the pews and the cobwebs that framed the ceiling fixtures.

Ryan turned to look at her. "You wouldn't think it by the looks of the place, but the altar gives an entirely different impression."

"Really?" she asked skeptically.

"Yes, really," Jack answered. "Come up here and take a look."

"I'm coming," she said, walking over to where the two men stood. "So show me what has you both convinced that there's been cult activity here."

Jack reached for the sheet that they had placed back over the altar when they had left earlier. "This," he said as he removed the sheet, exposing the pentagram beneath.

Ashley's hand automatically went to her throat. "Oh my."

Ryan gave her a sharp look. "What's the matter, Ashley? You look a little pale," he said in concern.

Ashley motioned to the pentagram. "That's not the same figure I showed you back at the apartment complex."

Ryan looked at her sharply before turning to stare at the five-pointed figure on the altar. "Are you sure? It looks like the same thing to me."

Ashley shook her head. "I'm positive. This one's inverted."

"So, what does that mean?" Ryan asked.

"It deals more with satanic worship than Wicca. That's what the symbol is referring to," she answered.

"You have to be kidding," Ryan said in disbelief.

She shook her head. "No. This is referring to black magic, not white."

"What's the difference?" Jack asked, curious despite himself.

"One refers to evil, and the other doesn't," she answered.

Ryan walked around to the back of the altar and removed the goblet that they had discovered earlier. "Do you know what this represents?"

Ashley nodded and walked closer. She picked up the goblet and studied it curiously. "It looks like an ordinary chalice. It's used in all religious ceremonies. But my guess is that this one was used to anoint the victim before the sacrifice was made."

"What makes you say that?" Jack asked as he walked over to where she stood.

Ashley reached into the rim of the cup and ran a finger around the brim. "The oil it contains."

"Great," Ryan replied.

Ashley looked over at him. "There's another problem, you know."

"What's that?" Jack asked.

"The witching hour is tomorrow night," she answered.

"And?" Ryan prompted, confusion evident on his face.

Ashley put the chalice back on the table. "The witching hour is the hour of midnight when there's a full moon. In the religion of Wicca, it's the time when the witches' spell-casting power is at its strongest. My guess is that there'll be another murder tomorrow night at midnight. There's a reason they're choosing these dates. I think the first two murders were just a prelude of what's to come."

Jack rubbed a tired hand over his eyes. "Great," he replied despondently.

Chapter Sixteen

An hour later, Jack and Ryan were headed back to the police station. Ashley had left in her own car to go back to the office.

As they drove along the expressway, a bolt of lightning streaked through the air, followed by the loud rumble of thunder. The daylight hours were beginning to fade, and dark clouds began to roll in from the east, promising another rainstorm.

"If the rain keeps coming like it has been lately, we won't have to worry about the wildfires this year," Ryan commented.

"We've been getting saturated lately," Jack agreed.

"Yeah. My basement is getting the overflow of water. I wish it would slow down just a bit. I don't have flood insurance," Ryan said.

"So far I've been lucky," Jack replied. "I haven't been getting any backlash."

"I wish I wasn't," Ryan said.

"Mm," Jack murmured, his thoughts beginning to drift to the vast knowledge Ashley seemed to have on the practice of Wicca.

"So what did you think of Ashley's theory?" Ryan asked, his voice filling the silence that was beginning to penetrate the car.

Jack laughed. "If it was anybody else, I would think they were crazy. But she seems to know just a little bit too much on the subject for my peace of mind," he admitted.

"I know what you mean. I felt chills on my neck when she began to talk about the witching hour," Ryan said.

"The part that bothers me is that she believes everything she said. It makes me wonder just how deep she was into it when she was covering that story," Jack said, reaching out to turn on the windshield wipers as the first drops of rain splattered the windshield.

"Did you ever read her article?" Ryan asked curiously.

"No."

"Do you want to?"

"What do you mean?"

"We can stop by the local library and go through the archives. I'm curious as to what she wrote."

Jack was silent for a moment before admitting, "To be honest, I'm a little curious too."

"So, do you want to stop?"

Jack turned to look at him, contemplating the question only briefly. "Sure. Why not?"

"Great. We can stop before going to the station. I'm sure Myers is going to want a full report on what we found today."

"I'm sure he will."

A half hour later, they were seated in the library going through old newspaper articles in the computer database.

"Did you find anything yet?" Ryan asked as he scanned one article after another.

"No, but it would help if we had a better idea of the date the article was printed. The only thing I know is the year it was written."

"Why don't you call Ashley and see if she remembers the print date?" Ryan suggested.

"And have her know that we're looking for a copy of the story? Are you out of your mind? I would never hear the end of it."

"Do you have a better idea?" Ryan asked.

Jack thought about the question seriously. "No, unfortunately I don't have a better idea. Though I wish I did."

"So call her. She'll probably be flattered that you're curious," Ryan said.

"I guess I have no choice," Jack said as he reached

for his cell phone and quickly dialed her number. After a brief conversation, he hung up the phone.

"What did she say?" Ryan asked curiously.

Jack gave a slight laugh. "She said if I wanted to read the story, I should have waited until I got home. Apparently she keeps a copy of all of her articles."

Ryan laughed. "Did she remember the date?"

"She remembered."

"What was it?"

"October thirty-first."

"Halloween," Ryan said.

"You got it."

"Figures."

"Mm. It should be in the next section," Jack said as he continued to scan. "I think I have it," he said, hitting the button to print out a copy of the article. He reached for it the moment it hit the paper tray and quickly read it.

Ryan watched the concentration on his partner's face as he read the article. "Well, what does it say?"

Jack continued to read the article, all of his attention focused on the contents. When he was through, his eyes were immediately drawn back to the section that had completely caught his attention. His forehead furrowed in a frown, he studied the words before him as he unconsciously began to slowly shake his head, denying what was in black and white.

Ryan became alarmed by his partner's silence. "Jack? What does it say?"

Jack slowly lifted his eyes from the paper. "She didn't just write an article on Wicca."

"What do you mean?"

Jack handed the article to Ryan. "She was initiated into the coven."

"I don't understand."

Jack ran a shaky hand over his face. "Read the article."

Ryan cast a concerned look at his friend before his eyes focused on the words before him. Shock held him immobile as he read Ashley's work. When he was through, he looked at Jack. "Ashley was more than initiated."

Jack was still trying to come to terms with what he had read. "I know."

Ryan looked down at the article once more, as if trying to confirm that he had read it correctly. "It says here that there are three levels in the hierarchy of the coven. The first one is the initiation. After you prove yourself worthy, you can advance to the second level."

"I read the article, Ryan. I know what it says," Jack reminded him.

Ryan shook his head. "But Jack, the article gave a detailed description of what takes place at the ceremony for the third level of the hierarchy. At the third level, a witch can become a high priestess or high priest."

Jack nodded and reached for the paper that Ryan held. He rubbed the back of his neck wearily, trying to ease the tension that had begun to build as he once again read the part of the story that bothered him the most. "I know. According to this, Ashley is qualified to be a high priestess."

Ryan shook his head in disbelief. "What are you going to do?" he asked as he watched Jack crumple the paper in his fist.

"I don't know yet."

"Are you going to talk to Ashley about what it says?"

"I have no choice," Jack said.

Ryan glanced at his watch. "It's early yet. Maybe you can catch up with her at her office."

Jack shook his head, knowing he had to come to terms with what he read before he could discuss it with Ashley. "No. I'll talk to her tonight. I need time to think about this. Right now, I want to head back to the station."

"Are you sure?"

"Yes, I'm sure. Come on, let's go."

Twenty minutes later they pulled into the parking garage at the station. Jack killed the engine and reached up to put the copy of Ashley's article into the slot between the sun visor and the roof of the car.

Ryan watched the action. "You don't want to show that to Myers?"

Jack shot him a look of disbelief. "You have to be kidding me."

"What do you mean?"

"It's bad enough I think my wife is somewhat of a

nutcase. I don't want anybody else getting the same impression."

Ryan laughed shakily. "She's not a nutcase."

"No?"

"No. She's just very dedicated to her career," Ryan said, defending her actions.

"Yeah, well, I consider myself dedicated too, but that doesn't mean I'm going to go out and commit a crime just to know how the criminal mind works."

"How can you say that? You commit a crime every-time you want to search a place without a warrant," Ryan reminded him.

"It's not the same thing," Jack denied.

"No?"

"No. Enough of this conversation. Let's go and see Myers," Jack said.

Ryan reached for his seat belt and released the catch. "Okay, let's go," he said, opening the car door and stepping out onto the concrete pavement of the garage floor.

Jack joined him. "What time did the crime scene technicians say that they would have the preliminary report?" he asked, trying to get his mind back to the job at hand. He needed to concentrate on solving this case. Tonight he would talk to Ashley and get the answers to his questions.

Ryan glanced at his watch. "It should be ready any minute."

"Good. I was kind of hoping to call it a day a little early tonight."

Ryan nodded. "Yeah, so was I."

"Let's hope everything goes as planned then," Jack remarked as they stepped into the elevator.

"Maybe some more information came in about the first victim, Lisa Baker," Ryan said, adjusting his tie as he looked into the mirrored panel on the wall.

"Hopefully. At the very least, we should have an identity on the latest victim. I would hate for it to be a Jane Doe."

"We didn't have the same crowd of observers on this one as the first."

"I know. I hate it when we have an audience."

"Sometimes it's good though," Ryan replied.

"Yeah? When?"

"When they can identify the victim," Ryan replied.

Jack inclined his head. "I'll grant you that, but that's the only concession that I'll make."

The elevator doors opened and Jack and Ryan exited the small enclosure. The station was surprisingly busy for late afternoon, and they saw several people talking to Myers in his office.

Jack walked over to the coffeepot and poured himself a cup of the thick brew. He took a gratifying sip before walking to his desk and taking a seat, hearing the springs creak as they took his full weight. "God, I'm tired," he said as he raised his feet to rest on the top of his desk.

Ryan opened a can of iced tea he had taken from the small refrigerator by the coffee maker. "I wonder who's in there with him," he said, gesturing with his chin to the people in Myers' office.

Jack shrugged. "It's anybody's guess."

"I hope they're not long."

"Why don't you call forensics and see if they came up with anything?" Jack suggested.

"Good idea," Ryan replied, reaching for the telephone.

Jack's eyes were closed while Ryan was talking on the phone, but he knew the moment he hung up the receiver. "Well?"

"The report is on its way over," Ryan answered.

"Did they I.D. the victim?"

"Yeah, they did. The girl's name was Liza Bentley. They ran a computer check on her and apparently she attended the same school as Lisa Baker," Ryan said.

Jack's feet hit the floor with a crash as he sat upright. "No kidding."

"That's what came in."

"There's something else they share," Jack said, his forehead creased in a frown.

"What's that?" Ryan asked.

"The same initials."

Ryan shook his head. "There can't be any connection because of that," he insisted.

"Maybe not, but it's interesting all the same. The report does prove one thing, however."

Ryan shook his head and reached for his drink. After taking a sip, he asked, "What's that?"

"The killer is familiar with the girls on campus. Did they manage to get an address on the girl?"

"We're about to find out," Ryan replied as a messenger delivered the sealed envelope.

Jack reached for it and tore the flap open. He scanned the contents thoroughly before handing it to Ryan.

"Her address is listed in the same building as the first victim," Ryan said as he read the contents of the report.

"I know. That means whoever our killer is knows the residents of that building very well," Jack said.

"It would lend a lot of credibility to Ashley's theory," Ryan replied.

"Yeah, it would. It still doesn't explain the motive though."

"There doesn't have to be a motive," Ryan said. "It could be that we're just dealing with a mentally ill person."

"Could be. It could also mean something else."

"Like what?"

"I don't know yet."

Ryan motioned to Myers' office. "It looks like they're wrapping it up in there."

"Good," Jack said standing. "Let's go and get this over with."

Chapter Seventeen

Jack was deep in thought on the way home, his mind on the article Ashley had written on witchcraft. He knew he was going to have to talk to her to find out why she felt the need to go so far in her research of Wicca. He needed to know what her mindset was on the subject. He needed to know if she actually practiced the religion. The authority she seemed to have on the subject bothered him more than he cared to admit. He couldn't help but wonder if the knowledge she had on Wicca came from actual practice and commitment to the religion rather than from research she did for the article.

As the darkness set, Jack automatically looked up into the sky at the moon. The white orb glowed into the night, almost full. His mind flashed back to what Ashley had said about the witching hour. If they were actually tracking somebody who fully believed in the powers of the moon, they might be able be able to nail the murderer tomorrow night. The thought was a slight comfort.

As Jack pulled into his driveway, he killed the engine and sat in the car looking at the house. His eyes shifted up to the second story, where the bedroom light beckoned. He was tired. The thought of going to bed early held infinite appeal, but he needed to talk to Ashley first. He needed to clear the air.

Opening the car door, he stepped into the chilly night air. He reached in the back seat for his suit jacket. Hooking it over one shoulder, he slammed the car door and headed up the walk.

He was just reaching for his house key when the door opened and Ashley stood silhouetted in the entrance, a black silk dress hugging her figure and a shawl draped over her arm.

"Hi," she whispered.

Jack stopped when he saw her. "Hi. You look beautiful," he told her honestly as he took in her appearance.

Ashley couldn't control the slight blush at his words. "Thank you. I was waiting for you to get home," she confessed, her eyes caressing his features.

"Were you?"

"Um-hmm."

Jack leaned against the porch railing. "We just saw each other a few hours ago."

"That's true."

"So?"

"So, I was kind of hoping we could go out for dinner tonight."

"Dinner?"

"Yes. We haven't really had a relaxing evening together since we got back from Hawaii."

Jack smiled at her. "We've only been back a couple of days," he reminded her gently.

"It seems longer," she confessed.

Jack knew what she wanted, and he was honest enough with himself to admit that he wanted it too. Ever since they got back from their honeymoon, the case he was working on seemed to take control of their lives, to the point of putting unwanted stress on the beginning of their married life.

"I know it does," he acknowledged softly.

"So, can we go? Just the two of us? No outside influences, no talking of careers. I just want to go out to be with you."

Although Jack was tired, he couldn't say no. They needed the time alone together, the time to unwind. They needed the time to talk. "Let me take a quick shower first."

Ashley nodded and stepped back to allow him to enter the house. "I'll wait in the living room."

Jack reached out to stroke her face, his fingertip just barely grazing her skin. "I won't be long."

The restaurant Ashley chose was small and secluded, on the Island's north shore. Their table was right by the window, with a view of the Long Island Sound. The only light came from the candlelit table and the moon and stars glowing in the night.

Jack looked around the restaurant with interest. "How did you find this place?" he asked curiously.

Ashley shrugged. "I used to come here a lot before I started seeing you," she admitted.

Jack's spine automatically stiffened at her words. "With who?" he asked, a tinge of jealousy lacing his voice. The restaurant seemed to cater to couples, not friends gathering for a social visit.

Ashley smiled. "Jealous?"

"Should I be?" he countered, not quite sure if he really wanted to know the answer to his question.

"No. You shouldn't be," she confessed.

Jack relaxed slightly at her words. "So who did you come here with?"

"Tom Black."

"You came here with Black?" he asked in disbelief.

"Yes," she said, frowning at his reaction. "Why do you sound so shocked?"

"Probably because I am."

"What do you mean?"

"I mean that I hadn't realized that you were seeing him outside the office."

Ashley shook her head. "I wasn't seeing him outside of the office," she denied.

"You weren't?"

"Of course not. Whatever gave you that idea?"

Jack shrugged and looked around the candlelit room. "The atmosphere in this place."

Ashley's eyes followed his gaze around the restaurant. "I don't understand what you mean."

"Ash, look around. This isn't the type of restaurant you come to for business meetings."

Ashley looked at him, a perplexed expression crossing over her face as the meaning of his comment sank in. "Jack, there was absolutely nothing going on between Tom and me."

Jack held out his hands. "Hey, calm down. I believe you. It's just that like I said, this doesn't strike me as an appropriate restaurant for business meetings."

Ashley looked around, acknowledging the truth in his statement. "It is a little intimate," she admitted.

"A little?" he asked, his voice expressing disbelief over her choice of words.

"Well, okay. It's very intimate. That's the reason I chose it tonight, actually."

"Hmm. Just out of curiosity, did you ever wonder why Black brought you here?"

"Why he brought me here?" she repeated with a shrug. "I guess because of the quality of the food. The filet mignon melts in your mouth," she admitted huskily.

"As long as you believe that," he replied with a shrug.

"I hope you're not suggesting that Tom was trying to make a pass or anything like that."

Jack frowned at the slight agitation in her voice.

"Hey, calm down," he soothed. "It's obvious from your reaction that he never succeeded, so you can relax."

"He and I are just friends," she insisted. "He is my boss, after all."

"I believe you," he assured her, regretting ever bringing up the subject. He reached for her hands, squeezing them gently. "Can we change the subject?"

Ashley stared at him a moment before smiling. "Of course."

"Good," Jack said, bringing one of her hands to his lips for a kiss. "I missed you today after you left."

Ashley's heart melted at his words. "Did you?" she asked softly, her eyes caressing his face.

"Yeah, I did. I wish I wasn't so involved with this case. Then we could have spent a few hours together, maybe had lunch."

"I would have liked that. I miss being with you too. I wish we were back in Hawaii. It was nice not worrying about anything other than what time to have dinner."

"If we both can get away, we'll go back there next year for our first anniversary. This time, though, we'll rent one of the condominiums we saw. It will give us a little more flexibility in what we want to do."

Ashley smiled. "That sounds wonderful."

"Yeah, it does," Jack said just as the waiter stopped by their table to ask if they were ready to order. After requesting a few more minutes, Jack looked over at

Ashley and picked up his menu. "I guess we should see what this place has to offer in the way of food."

"I guess we should," she responded.

Jack looked over the menu. "You recommend the filet mignon?"

"It's great," she acknowledged.

He nodded. "Good. That's what I'll have."

"You won't regret it," she promised as the waiter came back to their table.

Ashley waited until Jack placed both their orders before saying, "I know I promised that we wouldn't talk about our careers, but I'm curious. How did it go this afternoon after I left?"

Jack reached for the glass of scotch that the waiter had placed before him. He took a generous sip before saying, "All right, I guess."

"Just all right? Did you find my article?"

Jack nodded and put down his drink. "Yes, we found it."

"And? What did you think of it?" she asked, reaching for her own glass of wine to take a sip.

"Honestly?"

"Of course, honestly."

"I can't believe that you went to such lengths to research the subject," he told her flatly, deciding that the best way to get the topic out in the open was to come right out with it.

Ashley shook her head. "The only way to do research is to do it in depth," she replied.

"Yeah, but Ash, that was written from the point of

view of someone who believed in and practiced the craft."

She shrugged, unconcerned with his observation. "I have to admit that I was fascinated by the subject."

"To the point of progressing to the third level of the hierarchy? You were that interested in the subject?" he asked, his voice betraying a touch of skepticism at the cavalier way she explained her involvement.

Ashley didn't take offense at his questions. "What can I say? You should know me well enough by now to realize that I can't do anything by half measures. I could have stopped at just being initiated into the coven, I guess, but then I wouldn't have a full understanding of just what is involved in Wicca. I wanted to write the article from the point of view of somebody who lived the life on a daily basis. I wanted the public to understand the religion in its true sense."

"Yeah, well, you succeeded more than you'll ever know," he told her as he reached for his drink and took a sip. "Can I ask how you found out about the coven you did your research on? Or would that be revealing your source?"

"Actually, Tom told me about it."

Jack stiffened again at the mention of his name. "Black? Your editor?"

"Ex-editor. I work for Op-Ed now, remember?"

Jack smiled. "Stop it. You and I both know that your chances of keeping away from reporting aren't that great."

"Work with me here. I'm trying."

"I know you are, babe. And to be honest, it's not your reporting that bothers me as much as the type of stories you choose to cover."

"What does that mean? That if I covered the political beat, you wouldn't object?"

"No, I wouldn't object. The only reason I'm objecting so much now is because the stories you choose to cover are so dangerous."

"Your job is dangerous too, but I'm not complaining."

"It's not the same thing and you know it."

"But it is, Jack. Don't you see?"

Jack looked over at her, seeing the sincerity behind her words. "There's one big difference."

"What?" she asked.

"I have a gun and the ability to arrest anyone who steps out of line. The only thing you could do is ask for a quote."

Ashley smiled at his attempt to make light of the situation.

Jack reached for her hand. "Ashley, you have to understand. I love you. I made a vow to protect you at our wedding, and I took an oath to protect the public when I became a police officer. I can't just look the other way when you put yourself in danger."

Ashley squeezed his hand. "I know."

He searched her eyes, looking for some type of assurance that she understood where he was coming from. "We okay?"

"Yeah, we're okay."

Jack looked at her a moment longer. "I'm glad you understand."

"I do," she assured him softly, knowing that if their positions were reversed, she would feel the same way.

Jack smiled. "So tell me, how did Black know about the coven?"

Ashley shrugged, her forehead creased in a frown. "I don't know. He wanted the article to run on Halloween, so I just assumed that he heard about it from one of his sources. I don't think he counted on me taking as long as I did with the research though. I got the impression that he might have accepted a less detailed investigation so that we could have had the article print earlier. I know he wasn't thrilled with me when I told him that I would agree to write the story, if he would give me carte blanche with the length of time I felt I needed to accurately report my findings. I got the distinct impression that while I was after truth, Tom would have been happy just covering the sensationalism. I think I made him nervous when I told him that I wasn't going to stop after the initiation."

"Why didn't you stop after that?"

"Honestly?"

"Yes."

"I didn't feel that I had enough of a grasp on the topic to write a truthful article."

Jack nodded slightly. "And after the second progression?"

Ashley lifted one shoulder in a delicate shrug. "The same thing, I'm afraid. There was just something that

I wasn't getting out of the experience. I'd watch the other people in the coven, and there was this excitement, this electricity that surrounded them. And no matter how much I tried, I couldn't seem to capture it, at least not enough to do justice to an article about their religion. I felt I needed to be fair to them and what they held dear. For them, it's a way of life."

"So you went all the way," he said, beginning to get a better understanding of the woman he married. A better understanding of what she was capable of when she believed in something.

"Yes, I went all the way."

"Was Black happy with the end result?"

"I think so. I think now he's glad we did it on my terms."

"Why do you say that?" he asked curiously.

"I won a journalism award for the piece," she told him proudly. "And if I win an award for an article that Tom is the editor on, he gets some of the acclaim also."

Jack smiled at her. "It doesn't surprise me that you won an award. The article had a definite shock factor."

"I'm going to take that as a compliment, even though I'm not sure if that's how you meant it."

Jack laughed at her comment. "How did you locate the coven? Did Black introduce you to someone or did you manage to find them yourself?"

"Actually, it's funny that you ask. He gave me a lead to follow, but I actually made the contact. And let me tell you, it wasn't easy. It's not the type of religion where they welcome you with open arms. I guess they get too many thrill seekers who come more for curiosity than anything else. They're very particular about who they invite to join them."

Jack shook his head in disbelief. "I'd like to ask you a question, and I'd like an honest answer."

Ashley frowned at the seriousness of his statement. "You know I'll always be honest with you," she assured him softly, reaching out to touch his hand. "What did you want to know?"

Jack turned his palm up, capturing her hand in his. "I need to know if you practice Wicca," he said, his eyes holding hers captive as he tried to read her thoughts.

Ashley smiled. "Would it make a difference in our relationship?"

"Absolutely not. I just need to know."

Ashley studied him quietly for a moment, seeing the sincerity behind his words. "No, Jack. I don't practice."

"Truth?"

Ashley squeezed his hand reassuringly. "Truth," she told him just as the waiter brought the salads.

Jack waited until they were alone before he said, "I needed to know. I hope you understand."

"Of course I do," she assured him. "I would have asked the same question if our positions were reversed."

Jack nodded and reached for the salt and pepper. He sprinkled both liberally over his plate.

Ashley watched his actions with a raised eyebrow, but didn't comment. Instead she asked, "What are you going to do about tomorrow night?"

Jack didn't pretend to misunderstand. "You mean about the full moon and that stuff you said back at the cemetery?"

"Yes."

Jack sighed and shrugged his shoulder. "I don't know yet. If we had any idea where the guy was going to strike next, we would stake it out. But so far, the murders took place in two different cemeteries."

"You're forgetting one thing, though."

"What's that?"

"The church. It's being used for something other than Methodist services."

"I didn't forget."

"So?"

"So, maybe Ryan and I'll swing by tomorrow night and check it out."

"I thought you might."

Jack looked at her, a wry expression on his face. "Eat your salad."

Chapter Eighteen

The following morning, Jack met Ryan down at the station. Ryan was at his desk, eating a jelly donut and nursing a rapidly cooling cup of coffee, when Jack walked in.

"Morning," Jack murmured as he headed toward the coffeepot.

"Morning," Ryan returned around a mouthful of donut.

Jack poured himself a cup of the thick brew and took a seat behind his desk. He looked around him at the crowd of people going down the hallway. Motioning with his chin, he took a sip from his mug and asked, "Any idea on what's going on?"

"They busted a senator's kid last night on a DWI. The press caught wind of it and headed out here first thing."

Jack sighed. "Great."

"What's the matter?" Ryan asked, noticing the tension radiating from Jack's face.

"Nothing. Why?"

"No reason. You seem tense, that's all," Ryan replied.

Jack hid a yawn behind his hand. "Sorry. Rough night."

"Why? What happened?"

Jack shrugged. "Nothing. I just couldn't sleep because I was thinking about the case."

Ryan nodded. "I know how you feel. It's been getting to me too, lately. I thought for sure that we would have some type of lead by now."

"It'll come," Jack said. "How was your evening?"

"Okay. Yours?"

Jack shrugged. "Ashley wanted to go out to dinner last night."

"Oh? You didn't want to go?"

Jack ran a restless hand through his hair. "It wasn't that. She took me to a place that her editor, Tom Black, used to take her to."

"So?"

"The place isn't the type of restaurant that you would take a business colleague to," Jack said.

Ryan nodded his head slightly in understanding. "You think he was trying to put the moves on her?"

"I know he was. Problem is, she just didn't see it, or doesn't want to see it. I'm not sure which it is."

"Why does it bother you so much?" Ryan asked

curiously. "It's not like the guy is a threat to you or anything like that."

"No, I know that. There's just something about him that bugs me," Jack replied, leaning back in his chair and placing his feet on top of his desk.

Ryan finished his donut and reached for his coffee. After taking a sip, he said, "I can understand that. If it was my wife, I'd probably feel the same way." He paused for a moment before asking, "Did you talk to her last night about that article she wrote?"

"Yeah."

"And?"

"She had a reasonable explanation," Jack said, not wanting to go into the specific details of his conversation with Ashley.

"Good. I knew she would."

Jack smiled slightly at Ryan's faith in Ashley. "I thought we could stake out the old Methodist church tonight and see if anyone shows up," he said.

"You've been thinking about Ashley's theory that something's going to happen tonight, haven't you?"

"Yeah, I have. It wouldn't hurt to rule it out. God knows we have nothing else to go on right now. As much as the two murders are similar, there weren't any clues left behind to tie up the case, or even hint at a suspect. That makes me a little nervous. We should have something to go on by now."

"So what do you want to do this morning?" Ryan asked.

"I thought we could check out the original crime

scene again, see if there's anything that'll click after the latest murder. Maybe we can talk to the caretaker once more. I didn't buy his story that he saw nothing. Curiosity alone would have had him looking out from behind the curtains."

Ryan shrugged. "Oh, I don't know. I can understand not wanting to find out what was going on outside, especially in a cemetery."

"But that's just it, Ry. That's what this guy is paid to do. He's paid to watch the grounds, to make sure that nobody is robbing the graves, or destroying the property," Jack said.

Ryan nodded in resignation, accepting the truth of the words. "Okay. Let's go and see what we can find," he said, finishing the last of his coffee before rising from his desk.

"I'm right behind you."

It was later that afternoon when Jack and Ryan arrived back at the station.

"I can't believe we hit a total dead end with that caretaker," Jack stated as they walked through the door.

Ryan laughed. "He's a poor excuse for a watch-man."

Jack looked over at him in disgust. "The guy was bombed out of his skull and it wasn't even lunchtime. No wonder he didn't investigate the night of the murder. He was probably drunk that night too."

Ryan laughed outright. "You should have seen the

look on your face as he poured that can of beer over his corn flakes. It was priceless."

Jack ran a hand over his face, hiding a smile. "It was pretty disgusting."

"That it was," Ryan agreed just as the phone rang shrilly on his desk. He grabbed the receiver and listened intently.

"What is it?" Jack asked the moment Ryan replaced the receiver back into the cradle.

"That was the morgue. The family of our second victim is coming in this afternoon to make a positive I.D."

"They were able to trace them?" Jack asked.

"Yeah. They live in South Carolina. Apparently she was the only one of their clan who was in New York."

"Makes sense. She was attending school here, after all."

Ryan reached for a folder and opened it. "I wonder if they knew our first victim. They were never able to trace any of her family."

Jack leaned back in his chair. "It's possible. They were living in the same building and attending the same school."

Ryan nodded. "I'd like to be there when they identify the body."

"What time are they coming? Did they say?"

Ryan looked at his watch. "They should be here within the hour. I'm going to call the morgue back and ask them to call us as soon as they arrive," he said, reaching for the phone.

"While you're doing that, I'm going to take a walk down to the lab and see if they have anything we can go on."

Ryan looked up at him. "Okay."

"I'll see you in a bit," Jack said as he left the room.

Jack made his way to the elevator and pressed the DOWN button. He rocked back on his heels as he waited. Out of the corner of his eye, he noticed Tom Black speaking with Myers in the corridor by his office. His curiosity aroused, he left his spot and walked over to where the two men stood.

Myers looked up at his approach. "Jack. You know Tom Black, don't you?"

Jack looked over at Black and nodded. "We've met. What are you doing here?" he asked the other man.

Black shrugged. "I came to see if there was anything on the murders."

"I didn't realize you were working on the story," Jack replied.

Black shrugged. "I wasn't. At least not until Ashley told me that she couldn't cover it."

"You don't have another reporter that's capable?" Jack asked in disbelief. While he couldn't claim to know anything about the newspaper business, he did know enough from Ashley's remarks that Black didn't cover stories.

Black smiled. "You took away my best."

Jack didn't pretend to misunderstand. "I'm sure you understand why I would prefer that she not cover these assignments."

"Oh, I understand. I don't necessarily approve, but I understand. If she was mine, I would feel the same way," Black assured him.

Myers looked between the two men. "Is there something I'm missing here?" he asked.

"Nothing," Jack assured him with a brief glance in his direction.

Black laughed, but it held no humor. "That's not true," he told Myers. "Detective Reeves took away my star reporter."

Myers frowned. "Ashley?"

Black nodded. "Yes. Since their marriage, she has informed me that she can no longer cover the homicide beat. In the interest of her marriage, of course. But don't worry, I understand. It's just that I have to now pick up the pieces. And you have to admit that nobody can cover a story with the same zest as Ashley."

"I agree. I also know that she takes unnecessary chances when she's covering a story. A fact that doesn't appear to bother you in the least," Jack ground out.

Black shrugged. "My job is to get the stories, regardless of the consequences."

"And my job is to protect my wife," Jack stated calmly.

"I agree with Jack," Myers interrupted. "Ashley has no business covering this mess."

"It's moot point, since she has emphatically told me

that she won't be covering them any longer," Black pointed out.

Jack assessed him shrewdly. "So what's the real reason you're here? You never did answer my question."

"Didn't I?" Black returned.

"No."

"I apologize. I thought I had. As I was saying, Ashley had laid out the framework for this piece, and I thought it would be a shame not to follow through with it," Black said.

"What's your personal interest in it?" Jack asked, curious about the man's reply.

Black lifted an eyebrow. "I have no personal interest. My only interest in this story is that the public knows what's going on," he said, glancing at his watch. "And now, if you gentlemen will excuse me, I'm late for an appointment."

Jack and Myers watched him leave before Jack turned to Myers and asked, "What did you tell him?"

Myers shook his head. "Nothing. We didn't get the chance to talk before you came on the scene. It's strange."

"How?"

"When he first tracked me down, he seemed bent on getting the full story. He actually had the nerve to ask to see the files. But before I had a chance to read him the riot act, you came along. I guess I'm just surprised that he didn't persist a little more," Myers said.

"You weren't going to tell him anything, were you?" Jack asked.

Myers scoffed. "You should know better than to even ask that question," he chided.

Jack shrugged. "Just curious. The guy seems like he could be a charmer when he wants to be."

"What makes you say that?"

"He seemed to charm Ashley."

"Not enough to get her to cover the article," Myers pointed out.

"That's true."

"So where were you on your way to?" Myers asked.

"I wanted to take a walk to the lab and sort through the evidence."

"The second victim's family is coming this afternoon," Myers said.

Jack nodded. "I know. Ryan and I will talk to them."

"Good. I'll see you later then," Myers said as he turned and walked away.

Jack watched him leave before he turned back to the elevator.

Chapter Nineteen

Later that evening, Jack and Ryan arrived at the cemetery. Jack parked the car in a thicket of trees, obscuring it from sight. Dusk had just begun to fall, and the fullness of the moon illuminated the darkened sky, showing the shadows of the clouds as they floated past.

Ryan looked out, a grim expression on his face. "Cemeteries at night give me the creeps," he admitted.

A ghost of a smile played around Jack's mouth as he glanced at their surroundings. "I know what you mean."

"I just hope something comes of this tonight. I would love to put this one to bed," Ryan said, reaching out to roll down the window. The cool spring breeze floated into the car, along with the sound of the tree-tops rustling.

"So would I," Jack replied.

"I found something out today that I thought might be of interest to you," Ryan said as he released his seatbelt and made himself more comfortable.

Jack reached for his cigarettes and shook one out of the pack. Cupping his hand around his lighter, he lit the tip and inhaled before asking, "What's that?"

"Connie Myers' sister is married to Tom Black's brother."

Jack looked over at Ryan. "Connie Myers? The captain's wife?" he asked as he handed Ryan the cigarettes and lighter.

"That's the one," Ryan said as he lit his own cigarette.

"How did you find that out?" Jack asked curiously as he tried to digest the information.

"When I made the deli run this afternoon, I ran into the foursome coming out of the restaurant on the corner by the precinct. She seemed a little shell-shocked to run into me. I could tell it made her nervous."

"What did she say?"

Ryan shrugged. "What could she say? She had no choice but to introduce me. I mean, it's not like she could have pretended that she didn't know me."

"You think it's possible that she's the one who was feeding the police information to Ashley?"

"I think she's the one who was feeding information to Black. She's affiliated with several people at the station, in addition to being the captain's wife. I have little doubt that it wouldn't have been difficult for her to gain access to any information she wanted. She teaches police procedure at the academy. You know they like dealing with mock cases. What better way to get new recruits ready for the street than to simulate a real-life case. You know that nobody is going to deny her any information that she wants. Not as long as she's married to the captain."

"But why would she give Black information? What would she gain from it?" Jack asked.

Ryan shrugged. "There could be any number of reasons why she would do it. The most logical is that she was doing it as a favor for her sister and brother-in-law. Although it could be something else entirely different."

"Like what?"

"Maybe Tom Black charmed her into it. We won't really know until we talk to her."

Jack shook his head slightly. "You know what this means?"

"What?"

"Joe Myers may have inadvertently been the leak," Jack said as he leaned back in his seat and thought about the implications.

"You got it."

"I wonder why he never made the connection."

Ryan shrugged. "Probably because he trusts his wife. I would never had made the connection if I hadn't run into her with Black."

"Did you talk to Myers about it yet?"

"No. To be honest, I didn't get a chance. Plus I

wanted to run the theory by you. You know the woman better than I do. Is it possible that she would actually do something like this?"

Jack sighed. "Anything's possible."

"How do you suggest we approach it?" Ryan asked.

"What do you mean?"

Ryan gave a slight laugh, but it contained no humor. "How do you tell someone that their wife may have been giving out confidential information to the press? Especially someone in Myers' position? It's going to be a reflection off of him regardless of whether he personally had anything to do with it."

Jack nodded. "I see your point."

"Any way you look at it, it's a no-win situation."

Jack was about to speak when he heard the sound of a motor. "It looks like tonight might be our lucky night," he said to Ryan, motioning to the bright beams of light that were visible on the road.

The car stopped several hundred yards away, out of the immediate sight of where Jack and Ryan waited. The sound of mumbled voices could be heard as the occupants of the car exited the vehicle. It was the husky sound of one voice in particular that had the hair on Jack's neck standing on end.

Ryan looked over at him, an alarmed expression on his face. "That sounded like Ashley."

Jack had recognized her voice immediately. "That's because it's her," he said as he automatically reached for the door handle. "She promised me that she would stay out of this. She gave her word."

"Hey, Jack, calm down," Ryan interjected. "Maybe she has a logical excuse to be here. There are two voices drifting over. She's not alone."

Jack paused. He heard the second voice and suspicion shot through him. "No, she's not. It's my bet that Black is with her."

"But didn't he tell you down at the station this morning that she promised to stay out of it?"

"Yeah, he did. But Myers said he never actually got any information. If Ashley met with Black afterward, he might have been able to convince her to get the story after all."

Ryan looked over at him doubtfully. "I don't know, Jack. She knows how you feel about it."

"When has that ever stopped her before?"

Ryan was silent a moment, acknowledging the truth behind the words. "But still."

"But still, nothing," Jack returned grimly, his hand once again reaching for the door handle.

Ryan reached out a hand to stop him. "Jack, calm down and be reasonable. If you go rushing out right now, you're going to blow our cover. Think about it."

Jack took a deep breath and slowly released his grip on the handle. "You're right."

"Let's just see where they go. Maybe we'll be able to get a positive I.D. on the person she's with."

"I don't need a positive I.D.. Ten to one, it's Black."

"Let's be sure."

"Fine, we'll see where they go. But I'm telling you

right now, Ryan, the moment she enters that fence, I'm going after her."

"All right. Agreed."

The voices grew stronger as the two people crossed the road to the cemetery. It was obvious that the other person with Ashley was Tom Black.

"It's Black," Jack said as soon as his suspicions were confirmed. He watched as the two neared the fence and began to go over it. "She's going to go in. She's going to show him the way into the church," Jack ground out.

Ryan reached for his door handle just as a thought occurred to him. He turned to look at Jack. "You never did tell me this morning, and forgive me for asking, but when you spoke to Ashley last night, did she confirm or deny that she was practicing Wicca?"

Ryan's question stopped Jack cold. "What?"

"Is it possible that Ashley is an active member of a coven?" Ryan asked, hating to ask the question, but knowing that he had to.

"She denied it. Why?"

"It seems kind of strange that she would show up here."

Jack thought about Ryan's words. There was a grain of truth in them. He had spoken to Ashley last night regarding this cemetery and the church. She was too smart to show up at this site unless there was a reason for it. Was it possible that she was somehow involved in this mess?

Jack's silence alarmed Ryan. "Jack?"

Jack looked over at him. "Let's go and see what's going on."

"I'm with you," Ryan assured him.

Jack was already out of the car before Ryan finished his statement. He watched as Ashley took Black to the opening of the catacomb, and then disappeared from sight. He wasted no time in following.

Grabbing the top of the fence, he scaled it easily, landing on the other side with barely a thump. He waited impatiently for Ryan to perform the same maneuver.

"Let's go," Jack said softly into the still night, not wanting the sound of his voice to carry to the two occupants already underground. He knew from previous experience that they were just reaching the small door that led to the church.

They entered the catacomb and carefully made their way through the tunnel. As they came closer to the entrance to the church, the sound of voices could be heard from within.

It was only a few seconds before they came upon the wooden door that led up to the church. Relief washed over Jack the moment he saw that the hatch had been left open.

Jack carefully eased himself through the small opening, just enough to get a glimpse of the interior of the church without alerting anybody to his presence. What he saw absolutely chilled him.

It was the single candle burning in the middle of the pentagram on the altar that caught his eye first.

The sight stopped him cold. Several figures dressed in dark robes surrounded the altar, while the candle glowed evilly in a metal holder in the center of the ancient symbol.

The altar was surrounded with candles, the light casting an eerie glow around the room. Various hooded people were sitting in the pews, but it was the two people in black standing at the front of the altar that arrested Jack's attention. The hood had fallen off the person whose back was towards Jack, but he didn't need to see the face to recognize the individual. He would recognize her hair anywhere. It was Ashley. As shock ripped through him, the other figure turned toward him and lifted his face toward the ceiling. As the figure began chanting, the hood fell back, revealing the person beneath. It was Tom Black.

Jack silently stepped back down to the ground, his face ashen at what he had discovered.

"What did you see?" Ryan asked, frowning at the obvious pallor of Jack's skin.

"It's Ashley and Black at the front of the altar," he said, trying to come to terms with what he saw. The image of Ashley in a ceremonial robe was burned vividly in his mind, and he closed his eyes at the realization that Ashley could be standing before the altar as High Priestess of the coven.

"What are they doing?" Ryan asked.

"It looks like some sort of ceremony is taking place," Jack replied distantly, his thoughts in turmoil.

"How do you want to handle this?" Ryan asked,

praying that what was going on inside was totally innocent, but knowing the likelihood that it wasn't. Ashley was too smart too show up here unless she had a good reason. Ryan didn't think Jack was going to like what that reason turned out to be.

Jack looked over at Ryan. "She's my wife, Ryan."

"I know."

"I don't want her hurt."

Ryan nodded in understanding. "You want me to take care of it?"

"No. I have to do it," Jack replied grittily, already checking his gun to make sure it was fully loaded. "Cover me, will you?"

"What, are you kidding?" Ryan whispered. "I'm going in there with you."

"It's my wife."

"And you're my friend. If you go, I go. Besides, you said there were other people in there. You don't think that they're just going to let you waltz in there, do you?"

Jack rubbed the tension from the back of his neck. "You're right," he said, acknowledging the truth behind Ryan's words.

"I know I am. Let's get this show on the road," Ryan said, pulling his own gun out of his holster.

Jack looked at him for a moment, before saying, "Let's go."

Jack silently entered the church, Ryan right on his heels. The chanting was getting stronger, the robed figures' attention on the altar.

Jack and Ryan moved quickly to the side wall, fading into the shadows as they edged their way to the front of the church. A loose floorboard creaked, causing Jack to stop in his tracks with baited breath. Black turned at the sound, his eyes catching Jack's in the candlelight.

Black growled, a guttural sound from deep within his throat. "Reeves," he said as he caught sight of Jack.

"Black," Jack acknowledged, his full attention on the scene before him. He came out into the room, his eyes on Ashley, willing her to look at him.

Ryan managed to stay in the shadows, his gun cocked and ready to fire. He held his breath as he watched the scene unfold.

Black shook his head. "You shouldn't have come here tonight."

Jack ignored his words. "Ashley," he called out, trying to get her attention. He wanted to look into her eyes, to see if she was aware of what she was doing. He wanted to see her face.

"She won't answer you," Black said.

"Ashley!" Jack shouted in desperation. He wanted her to look at him, he wanted her to acknowledge the insanity of the situation.

Black looked at him, his face devoid of any expression. "She no longer belongs to you, she belongs to us. She stands proudly here tonight as we begin the celebration of the uniting of the God and Goddess."

"The Goddess?" Jack repeated, suspicion racing

through him like wildfire as the words of her article flew through his mind.

"She will give herself to the God tonight as a sign of loyalty to our coven. She will offer herself in body and in spirit. Her blood will be a testament to her fidelity, the giving of her life will be her pact. They will be united for all eternity."

Jack's eyes flew to Ashley while his mind denied what was being said. "No."

"She's already accepted the doctrine," Black replied as he motioned for the two followers on either side of Ashley to turn her in the direction of Jack.

Jack looked at Ashley and shook his head, denying what he saw. Her eyelids were at half-mast, her head rolling back on her neck. Dark rage filled him the moment he realized she had been drugged. "What have you done to her?" he ground out, leaping from his place toward Black.

The robed figures began rushing toward Jack, but he was livid with rage. He managed a flying tackle on Black, bringing him hard to the ground, as his fist continually met the flesh on the man's face.

When Jack felt somebody try to grab his arms, he let out a bellow of rage. Fighting with the people who were trying to pull him off Black, he managed to grab his gun, holding it to the other man's temple.

"Tell them to back off!" he demanded of Black, whose face had turned a deathly white at feeling the cold steel of the gun.

When the man refused to say the words, Jack's anger exploded. He felt himself pull back on the trigger, his eyes wide and filled with rage.

"Jack!" Ryan shouted, a moment before gunfire exploded in the air.

Jack looked down at his victim, sanity slowly returning. Though the gun was still pointed at Black's temple, it wasn't his gun that had fired. It was Ryan's.

"All of you, just stay back," Ryan shouted, coming out of the shadows, his gun spanning the room.

Black looked up into Jack's enraged features. "You can kill me, but my people will kill Ashley. Either way, she will be united with her destiny tonight," Black promised darkly.

Jack kept his gun trained on Black, but lifted his head to look across at Ashley. One of the robed figures supporting her held a silver dagger to her throat.

Jack looked back at Black. "Tell them to let her go!" he demanded.

"Her fate awaits," Black decreed.

"Her fate is with me," Jack ground out, lifting his arm and taking aim at the man that held the knife. His aim was precise, his thoughts deadly. With one pull of the trigger, he hit Ashley's assailant in the arm, watching as he dropped her to the ground and doubled over in pain. The action had been instinctive and quick. Nobody had anticipated his move. The other person that had held Ashley's arm ran to the other side of the room, joining the crowd of robed figures cowering in the corner. Nobody else seemed inclined to join the fray.

The moment Ashley lost her support, she crumpled to the ground. Jack's eyes immediately made contact with her throat, reassuring himself that she had not been cut.

Turning back to Black, he held the gun back to his temple. "It's a shame that you don't believe in God. Because sure as night follows day, you're about to meet your maker."

"Jack!" Ryan shouted, trying to bring some sense of sanity back to his partner.

Ryan's voice penetrated Jack's rage and his eyes began to focus. He looked down at Black, noticing the pallor of his skin that now glistened with sweat. The smell of fear permeated the air around him.

"Jack," Ryan repeated. "Think about what you're doing. If you kill him now, it will be premeditated. You won't walk away. Don't throw away your life over him," Ryan begged.

Though the rage was still there, Jack's self-control started to kick in. His eyes drifted over the occupants of the room, noticing the fear on the faces of Black's followers as they tried to distance themselves from the scene unfolding. He took a deep breath and mentally counted to five. All of his instincts told him to take this man out of the picture. Permanently. But common sense told him Ryan was right. He wouldn't walk away from this.

With his gun still trained on Black, he slowly lifted himself off of him, watching the relief cross the man's features.

"You're not worth it," Jack told him before turning to Ryan. "Watch him, will you?"

Ryan immediately came over to Black, his handcuffs out. "I have him," he assured him.

Jack nodded and shakily made his way over to where Ashley was. He took her prone body in his arms and carried her over to one of the pews, laying her down. Gently pushing her hair away from her forehead, he looked down at her face. She was unconscious.

"Is she all right?" Ryan asked, concern etched in his features as he finished handcuffing Black.

"She's out of it," Jack replied, lifting her eyelids and noticing the dilated pupils, the unevenness of her breathing.

"I radioed for backup. They should be here momentarily," Ryan promised, lifting Black to his feet and pushing him toward the other people in the room.

Jack nodded, all of his attention focused on Ashley. He didn't respond to Ryan's statement. He was looking at Ashley, trying to find some indication that she would be okay.

"She'll be all right, Jack," Ryan said, trying to reassure him.

"She'd better be," Jack replied, his eyes turning towards the group of followers as he was overcome with an anger so intense, he didn't know if he would be able to contain it.

"She will be," Ryan said.

Chapter Twenty

It was early morning when Jack and Ashley let themselves into their house. After Ashley regained consciousness, she had been checked over at the hospital, just to ensure that there would be no lasting damage from the drug she had been given. Ryan had promised to complete the paperwork down at the station, while Jack took Ashley home.

"I still can't believe that Tom would be involved with something like that," Ashley said for what seemed like the hundredth time.

Jack removed his suit jacket from around her shoulders. "He was mentally sick, babe."

"I realize that. But to kill two people? What possible motive could he have had?"

Jack shrugged. "From what we could gather, the two victims wanted out of the coven. Problem was, they knew too much about his plans. Black may be a lot of things, but he isn't stupid. There was no way he would leave any loose ends lying around. There was no way he would accept that type of betrayal from his followers."

"But I don't understand why he would involve me in this whole sordid mess," she said.

Jack moved over to her and took her in his arms. "You represented his ideal woman. I think that he honestly believed that you would be the ultimate gift to his god. You already proved yourself to him when you did the story on Wicca."

Ashley hugged Jack, drawing strength from his strength. "But I never gave him any encouragement that I wanted to join the coven. It was just a story."

"He didn't need any encouragement. The scene had already played out in his head. His fantasy became his reality."

"Maybe. But it's hard to come to terms with what happened," she told him, burrowing into his warmth.

"I know."

"I'm glad you were there."

"So am I. But I have to admit, you scared the living daylights out of me," he said, his voice husky with emotion.

Ashley sank into his embrace and closed her eyes. "I was terrified tonight," she admitted.

"I know."

"What do you think will happen to him?"

"To Black?"

"Mm."

"The man killed two people, Ash. The state would be within their rights to seek the death penalty."

"I know," she sighed. "And it's not that I don't think he should have to pay. It just seems so strange when it's somebody that you know, somebody that you trusted."

Jack nudged her. "Come on. Why don't you go sit on the sofa and I'll get us a drink."

"Okay."

"What would you like?" Jack asked.

Ashley shrugged, watching as he walked across the living room to the small bar set up in the corner. "Whatever you're having."

"Scotch?"

"That's fine," she said and then watched as he poured himself a healthy measure of scotch and belted it back in one swallow. He refilled his glass before pouring out a small measure for her.

Jack came back to the sofa and sat down beside her. He pressed the glass into her hand. "Here you go."

Ashley took a sip and grimaced as the fiery liquid slid down her throat. "I'm glad we're home."

"Me too, babe," Jack said as he took a sip of his own drink. "Do you feel up to talking?"

Ashley settled against his side, her head resting against his shoulder. She felt his lips on the crown of her head as his arm went around her, and she closed her eyes in contentment. "Sure. What did you want to talk about?"

"I was wondering, what made you go with Black tonight?"

Ashley shrugged, trying to think of the best way to explain the circumstances to him. "He had called me earlier, begging me to help him with this one story. I knew he had gone to the station, trying to fit together the pieces to run the article in tomorrow's edition. He said that you were there, charging like a bull in a china shop, and he was unable to lay any groundwork," she told him with a slight smile. "And since that sounded exactly like what you would do, there was no reason for me to doubt him."

"He was trying to con Myers into giving him information," Jack admitted, not taking offense at her choice of words.

"It's his job," she said matter-of-factly.

"He couldn't get the information from Connie Myers?" Jack asked.

Ashley glanced at him sharply. "You know?"

Jack shrugged. "Ryan ran into them coming out of a restaurant."

"Does her husband know?"

"He probably does by now. Ryan went to meet with him. But enough about that. Tell me how you got involved tonight," he said, his hand absently stroking her arm.

"When Tom called me tonight, he asked about the second cemetery. I had let it slip about the catacomb," she replied, her voice containing just a hint of an apology.

"Accidentally, I hope."

"Accidentally," she confirmed with a grimace.

"And he somehow conned you into showing him where it was," Jack concluded, taking a sip of the drink that he held in his hand.

"Please understand, Jack. I couldn't say no. I had somehow started the story after all. I had no idea that he was really behind the whole mess."

"I know you didn't, Ashley," Jack told her soothingly. "It's just that I don't know what I would have done if something had happened to you."

"I was only going to show him the catacomb. I wasn't planning on staying. But once we got into the tunnel, I heard voices. I knew you and Ryan weren't inside, so I had a pretty good idea of what we were about to walk in on. What I didn't know was that Tom had orchestrated the whole thing. I had no idea what he had planned. I never had a clue. I thought of Tom as a friend. It was because of him that I got my first break in reporting."

"With friends like that, you don't need enemies."

She moved suddenly, shifting her weight so that she sat on his lap. Removing the glass from his hand, she set it down on a nearby end table. "No," she agreed. "With friends like that, I don't need enemies."

She leaned further into him and closed her eyes, enjoying his closeness. Jack's arms tightened around her as thoughts about what could have happened flew through his mind. "God, Ashley. When I think about what could have happened," he began.

"Nothing did," she reminded him softly, reaching up to kiss his jaw.

"It could have."

"But it didn't," she told him soothingly.

They sat there quietly for a few moments, before Ashley spoke. "I have no idea of what I'm going to do with my time."

"What do you mean?"

"My career at the newspaper is over, Jack. I couldn't go back to work for them after this."

Jack looked down at her upturned face and traced a finger over her lips. "I don't want you to give up your career. That was never my intention. I only want you to be safe."

"I know. And I will be. But for now, my life is with you. I can get another job writing. The city is full of magazine publishers. I can get a job with one of them when I decide to go back to work."

"You won't be happy doing that," he insisted.

"Yes, I will," she insisted. "But for now, maybe we can get started on a family?"

"A family? As in kids?" Jack asked, slightly stunned by the change in topic. It wasn't one that they had talked about before.

"I'd like one," she told him softly.

"Just one?" he asked, the beginnings of a smile playing around his mouth.

Ashley leaned toward his mouth to kiss him. "Or two, or three," she whispered.

"Three, huh?"

"Unless you have another number in mind?" she asked him teasingly.

"Maybe we should sleep on it," Jack said, rising from the chair and lifting her into his arms.

Ashley wound her arms around his neck as he carried her to the stairs and up to their room. "Maybe we should," she agreed.

"At least we can agree on something," Jack told her teasingly as he entered the bedroom and kicked the door closed. He carried her over to the bed and laid her down.

"I always knew we would," she murmured huskily.

"You did, huh?"

"I did."